The BREATH of LIFE

DONALD E. CARR

The BREATH of LIFE

W · W · NORTON & COMPANY · INC ·
NEW YORK

TO MILDRED

The BREATH of LIFE

The BREATH of LIFE

. . . . dust of the ground
And in thy nostrils breathed
The breath of life
In His own image.

Milton, *Paradise Lost*

Introduction

. . . and chemistry anneals the common clay.

DAVID MCCORD, *Ballade of Time and Space*

To the average 140 I.Q. reader (a diligent subscriber to *The New Yorker* or *Daedalus,* for example) nothing is so deadly as chemistry. There is something about this science that casts an immediate pall. A woman married to a chemist is at a disadvantage, except with wives of other chemists, because the mere mention of her husband's profession brings uncontrollable yawns. In the American spirit, chemistry has established itself as the champion bore of all bores.

Why should this be? It is easy to accept the Charles Snow opinion that humanity is divided into scientists and non-scientists and that chemistry as a science shares its onus of boredom among the non-scientists with its sister disciplines. This is obviously not quite true, since biology can always make the first page with a story on birth control or the plight of the birds.

I am, however, sanguine enough to believe that a dissertation on the chemistry of the air and the way chemicals in the air can ruin us may interest the non-scientific reader. Some of my fellow scientists may not regard this as a dissertation but as a highly personal diatribe by a screwball from Los Angeles, and perhaps they will be right.

In my defense as a professional chemist, I must state that for many more years than I should like to own up to, I have been concerned at a technical level with the problem of air pollution. If this book seems slanted more to the weird dilemma of Los Angeles than to Dubuque, that is deliberate, since I must

[13]

regard Los Angeles as the all too well developed chemical hand-
writing on the wall and as a portent of things to come for the
motorized centers of population of the modern world. The
problem of Tokyo, for example, is of the same kind and is
perhaps even worse.

No pretense in this book is made to encyclopedic coverage
of the whole air-pollution problem, which would involve, for
example, a consideration of the dust from pigeon droppings in
New York City and San Francisco, all the way to small amounts
of beryllium from the scrapping of burnt-out fluorescent lamp
tubes. Indeed, the main thesis of the book can be taken to be
that, compared to fouling of the air by the burning of carbonaceous fuels, all other sources of pollution are either so puny
that they can be ignored or they are so easily controlled by
appropriate local action that no national problem except one
of simple enforcement really exists. One can prevent a Donora
catastrophe, for example, by simply requiring that the emission
of sulfur dioxide to the atmosphere by zinc plants be stopped
by the installation of appropriate absorbers. This is not true
of fuel-burning (of coal in London, for example) and, above
all, in the case of the automobile in large urban centers in geographic situations that are subject to atmospheric inversions,
where the problem is a desperate one for which I have suggested
some perhaps unpalatably desperate remedies.

It may be fair to the reader to explain that a certain amount
of journalism is involved in the writing of this book; and it may
be instructive to explain how I became a chemist. At one time,
at the age of eighteen I was working as a cub reporter on the
Portland *Oregonian,* and the salaries were far from princely.
I remember that the star reporter, a lovable, exuberant fat guy
whose joy was fishing for steelhead trout, got forty-five dollars
a week, and this seemed to the rest of us peons an incredible

reward, although at the time of the Astoria fire he had two by-line stories on the front page at the same time. At such wages as mine, one eats what used to be called in Portland "thin steaks" (razor-cut gristle fried in stale grease). I became very ill and went through a period vacillating between a desire to ship out to Singapore and a constant fear of death. Perhaps I should not say a fear, but rather a violent disinclination. Like Boy'yub's philosophic clerk, I figured I would rather burn forever in hell than simply become nothing. This impelled me to the idea (not a new one, but it seemed so to me at the time) to conquer death by sheer cunning. Hundreds of smudgy pages that have since been devoured by mice were at this time produced by me relating to what I termed in my little notes to myself "artificial encephalization." The general idea was to preserve the head and the brain, indefinitely, in a broth of nutrients, long after the liver, the bowels, and the heart had been decently interred or given to the cats. Thus one would be able to survive indefinitely as a head.

It occurred to me, however, as time went on, that I knew nothing at all about biological chemistry. How does a head get by, all by itself? Is the poor thing simply subject to the most famous ventriloquist gag of history ("All right?"—"All right!")?

I persuaded my patient father to send me to Berkeley to learn biological chemistry. Berkeley since my sojourn there has become a sort of scientific principality. One stumbles over innumerable Nobel prize winners in Faculty Glade and, in a rather serious sense, Berkeley runs the western world, through its tentacles at Los Alamos, the Radiation Laboratory and through its numerous powerful subsidiaries in San Diego, Westwood, Santa Barbara, Riverside, Santa Cruz, the "Farm," and at Irvine. But at that time Berkeley didn't know anything of use to me in biological chemistry. They had never considered the problem of "All right?—All right!" In fact, as I proceeded through my rather desperate freshman and sophomore years I concluded with growing apprehension that not only biological chemistry but chemistry itself were junior sciences.

There was, however, a great chemist there by the name of Gilbert Lewis, a cigar-chewer and an authentic genius. I recall that he invited a wild-haired, big-eared blond Oregonian boy from Cal Tech to give a seminar, and we chemist seniors were exposed to the chalk-dust and the irresistible scientific charm of Linus Pauling. Another whale in this puddle was an eccentric Englishman by the name of Dirac, who dazzled us with a new way of thinking about physical chemistry. Chemistry by that date had embarked upon its thrilling modern phase. The "quanta" had arrived and henceforth the science would never be the same and the facts and theories would subsequently be slightly incomprehensible to all but the initiated.

I was hooked. I never found out how to make a disembodied head that would survive through the centuries to come, but I had reached the conclusion that chemistry was important fun.

The problem of modern air pollution is indeed chemistry at its outer limits. If in this book on that problem I can convey some of the riotous urgency and the frantic meaning of chemistry to an all-important segment of our lives, I shall be satisfied.

chapter 1

THE NATURE OF AIR

. . . This most excellent canopy, the air.

SHAKESPEARE, *Hamlet*

The human race had air pollution problems long before it understood what air was made of. London was badly fouled with coal smoke at a time when the eighteenth-century chemists were starting to get rid of the "phlogiston" theory, which explained burning as the release of a mysterious substance rather than the reaction of oxygen with things that will burn. The discovery of oxygen by Priestley and Lavoisier was one of the most thrilling intellectual adventures of man. It took the human race immediately out of the doldrums of alchemy, just as the findings of Copernicus, Galileo, Newton et al. had rescued the race from astrology.

Everything in the day-by-day chemistry of living suddenly began to make sense. And yet some two centuries later we are beginning to realize that, in spite of its engaging show of simplicity and lack of guile, air can become enigmatic and even treacherous.

Suppose we change the composition of air for special purposes of our own; let's say, in order to fly in a capsule to the moon. For engineering reasons, it is much better to design such a capsule for pure oxygen at low pressures rather than to drag along a cabin full of classical air of 79 per cent nitrogen content at normal pressures. This sounds fine, since we have used pure oxygen to whiff at high altitudes in airplanes; we use oxygen to try to revive terminal cases of pneumonia, heart disease, and the like; and we have used oxygen to snap us out of hangovers. But how is it for a steady diet?

This question has precipitated between the National Aeronautics and Space Agency and various space medical authorities a bitter, noisy row. The M.D.'s accuse the agency of sacrificing health and safety to engineering expediency. Prolonged exposure to pure oxygen at low pressures is said to produce partial loss of eyesight, anemia, and other ills. Moreover, it is a precarious medium to do one's little tasks in, because of a curious effect that should have been foreseen but was overlooked. This is the "saturation effect" and it may be understood from a series of experiments the Navy carried out at Point Mugu, California, on living in low-pressure oxygen.

One of the sailors in the experimental cell sought to replace a burned-out electric light bulb and, because the old bulb was hot, he applied a towel to unscrew it. The towel immediately burst into flame. He tried to beat the flames out with his hand, and his hand burst into flame. He tried to beat his hand out against his trouser leg and his trouser leg caught fire.

This frustrating experience was caused by the fact that everything of an organic chemical nature in the cell (towel, flesh, trousers) was saturated with oxygen. The spontaneous-ignition temperature was already much lowered in pure oxygen, but the oxygen absorbed on the organic surfaces additionally provided a sort of kindling effect. Edna St. Vincent Millay's "lovely light" thus could be achieved much more simply in such an atmosphere, and life would become more dramatic, if shorter.

It is true that most of the disagreeable surprises of air are caused by things we do to it, and this will be the subject of this book. However, there are certain basic instabilities in the structure of the atmosphere which can be a source of worry, if one

[18]

has several millennia to spend worrying. Let us note just one, for the time being.

At very high altitudes there is a radiation chemical reaction involving protons or hydrogen ions of high energy which come from the sun in periodic swarms. In this reaction the nitrogen of our atmosphere undergoes a nuclear transformation to give the carbon isotope, C^{14} (which forms the basis of all radiocarbon "dating"), and it was originally assumed that the atmospheric end-product was carbon dioxide—a necessary ingredient of the atmosphere. It is now believed that this reaction does not produce carbon dioxide but produces carbon monoxide.

Why aren't we all dead? One reason is that certain plants and especially a soil bacterium *B. oligocarbophilus* can convert carbon monoxide to carbon dioxide. Without the luckily perverse appetite of this bacterium, one might expect that over a period of centuries the surface-level atmosphere would become definitely toxic from this cosmic synthesis, especially since carbon monoxide is an obstinately stable compound (except in its vicious reaction with the blood cells of warm-blooded animals) and does not undergo the slow, cushioning solubility processes in the oceans which serve to maintain the carbon dioxide balance on earth. Thus carbon monoxide (and moreover in a radioactive form) would tend to build up indefinitely.

What if our perverse bacterium falls by the wayside because of some evolutionary accident or perhaps is poisoned obscurely out of existence? This could be the way the world ends, in a prolonged whimper of carboxyhemoglobinosis.

Aside from such an inscrutable piece of planetary bad luck, for beings such as us, the present air that Nature has presented is a masterpiece of chemical balances. It seems to have been formed roughly in the following way:

The Sun probably was born in a whole shower of stars, and in the process of the Sun's formation (a sort of agglutination of clouds of hydrogen and heavier atoms from previously exploded, older stars), the Sun went through a phase which seems to be common to the birth of suns throughout the universe: as it contracted, it whirled faster until the centrifugal force threw out a disk. This is as if an ice skater, whirling faster and faster with his arms folded, suddenly lost control of his shirttail and it whirled about his middle. The whirling shirttail is the disk out of which the planets were formed.

Once the Sun had grown a disk, there was a steady transference of rotational momentum from the Sun to the disk. Two important things resulted. The Sun was slowed down to its present slow rate of spin (just as the ice skater's whirling shirt would slow his whirl) and the disk, containing the material out of which the planets were later to condense, was pushed farther and farther from the Sun. The solar condensation probably first grew its disk when it had shrunk to a size somewhat less than the orbit of the innermost planet, Mercury. The pushing outwards of the main bulk of the disk explains why the larger planets lie so far from the sun.

What then happened to make the good green earth and the other planets and satellites out of this whirling gaseous shirt? Before the shirt reached the distances of the great planets, such as Jupiter, Uranus, and Saturn, the higher melting and heavier materials became condensed out of the gas as a swarm of solid bodies. This is why the inner planets, including Earth, are smaller and made up of rock and iron—simply because the rock and iron were the first important materials to separate out of the gas. Beyond the inner planets water and ammonia were able to condense out of the gas and this represented the first phase in the building of these gigantic outer planets which are composed mainly of water and ammonia with some hydrogen attracted from space by the large gravities of these monsters.

What was the early Earth like? It is an astonishing conclusion of modern geochemists and biologists that life probably existed on earth before there was any appreciable nitrogen, carbon dioxide, or oxygen in the atmosphere. In other words, life, of a sort, preceded what we have come to know now as the very breath of life. The primitive atmosphere, a mere gaseous skin on the rocks and the oceans (which were squeezed up to the surface during the creation of the earth's core and mantle), contained hydrogen, water vapor, ammonia, and methane. This seems to have been the nature of the atmosphere for at least two billion years. This gaseous mixture is sensitive to strong ultraviolet light, against which we are now fortunately protected. The combination of powerful ultraviolet radiation with hydrogen, water, ammonia, and methane proved to be a good environment for making the complex molecules, such as amino acids and porphyrins, which are a sort of prelude to living organisms. This has been confirmed by recent laboratory experiments.

Since there was no early oxygen in the early atmosphere to react with them, the organic compounds that were formed continued to accumulate for millions of years. Only the ultraviolet radiation itself could have destroyed them and prevented the formation of even more complex molecules by eventually breaking them up again. The establishment of an equilibrium between photochemical synthesis and breakdown was probably postponed by the protective action of the oceans in which these building stones of life, the amino acids, are easily dissolved. As Nobel laureate Harold Urey has pointed out, if half the present surface carbon existed as soluble organic compounds and only 10 per cent of the water of the present oceans existed on the primitive earth, the ancient oceans would have been approximately a 10 per cent solution of organic compounds. This would provide a very favorable sort of soup for the origin of life.

No free oxygen could have existed in the earth's air as long as hydrogen was the prevailing molecule. But hydrogen is a very light gas, and the earth's gravity over a period of eons was not strong enough to prevent the gradual escape of hydrogen into outer space, just as all gases of any kind escaped the still weaker gravity of the moon. During this period of hydrogen escape, oxygen was formed in traces by the direct decomposition of water and later in large amounts by the action of green plants.

There must have been a long interim period on earth of very spectacular thunderstorms, since lightning would have caused occasional vast explosions of hydrogen-oxygen mixtures in the air. In fact, oxygen lived a precarious existence until the hydrogen had taken flight. When there was sufficient oxygen for it to become a stable component, the atmospheric ammonia was oxidized to nitrogen and the methane to carbon dioxide. Now a phenomenon of extraordinary beneficence took place. The embryonic world of life became protected against the swords of ultraviolet light which made life possible in the beginning but which then slashed away at the basic chemistry necessary to the continued development and proliferation of life. Oxygen began to react in the upper levels of the atmosphere to form ozone, which in turn absorbed the most damaging of the ultraviolet rays from the Sun.

In early geologic times green plants flourished with a magnificence impossible to visualize today but which can be estimated from the astronomical deposits of coal, which is fossilized primitive plants. In a much hotter world than we know now, even in our tropical jungles, the green plants gulped up the carbon dioxide which was then present probably in much greater concentration than now and which contributed to the worldwide tropical climate (due to the "greenhouse effect," which we shall presently describe). When the carbon dioxide was reduced in amount because of the voracious appetites of plants, the fierce honeymoon was over, and the planet settled down for several hundred million years to a more temperate existence, favoring such relatively delicate creatures as the mammal Man. The air at the end of the Carboniferous era was probably not very different than it is today some 500 million years later. It is the mammal Man who is now changing the air.

Now life "had it made." The rest of the job of stabilizing the air to a composition roughly as we know air today was up to the green plants.

One note should be added in regard to the ability of plant life to produce oxygen. Only recently it was discovered that the evolution of oxygen is a reaction rather separate from the photochemical decomposition of water and assimilation of carbon dioxide which together are the basis of the crucial process of photosynthesis which made plant life possible as a sort of parasite on plant life. Oxygen evolution depends on the catalytic action of *manganese*. If manganese is withheld from growing plants, their photosynthetic process becomes incomplete and similar to that known to occur in certain primitive, light-dependent bacteria. These "purple bacteria," so-called because of their color, do not use oxygen (they are "anaerobic"). They reduce carbon dioxide in the light while oxidizing a great variety of inorganic and organic substances, such as molecular hydrogen or acetate, but they never release a trace of free oxygen. Purple bacteria may serve as a model of an evolutionary step just below that of the green plant. The lucky combination of the right porphyrin derivative with a special manganese-protein complex has led to the result which created those free oxygen conditions that in turn made Darwinian evolution possible.

It should never be forgotten that the atmosphere is not only our breath of life, but it is also our protective coating against the ruinous high-energy radiation of the Sun. As mentioned above, if it were not for the formation of ozone at altitudes of 15 miles by one set of ultraviolet rays and the simultaneous destruction of ozone by another set, we would be naked to this blistering bombardment and would quickly perish. Ozone is the fall guy, screening out these lethal radiation bands both during its birth and destruction. This steady-state existence of ozone in the "ozonosphere" is ironically our salvation while at ground level, as will be shown later, it is becoming one aspect of our ruin because of man's increasingly massive pollution of the air. This is typical of the chemistry of air—the protean nature of its components. They are chemically busy in so many directions.

Even nitrogen, which has been regarded through most of man's modern history as chemically inert, was never actually so, for if it were not for the ability of nitro-bacteria to "fix" nitrogen (convert it into forms which plants can absorb) there would be no life on earth. Yet since Fritz Haber in 1915 invented a process for artificially fixing nitrogen to make ammonia and nitrate fertilizers, we have realized that a process of nitrogen fixation takes place in every high-temperature burning process. The fixation of nitrogen in automobile engines is perhaps the chief cause of Los Angeles smog.

Carbon dioxide in normal air seldom exceeds a concentration of thirty-three thousandths of one per cent. Since, with water it is the basis of all biological synthesis of wood, cellulose, sugars, starch and to a large extent of proteins, it is essential, of course, to life. However, this vital compound also has its dangers.

Because carbon dioxide is absorbed by plants in the process of photosynthesis, the air near the floor of a forest covered with rapidly growing vegetation on a bright summer day may be only one-third of the normal value (it has been suggested that crops may be forced to unheard-of abundance by artificially increasing the carbon dioxide concentration of the air over them). On the other hand, near the floor of a forest covered with decaying leaves and in the absence of bright sunlight, the carbon dioxide content may be three times the normal value. The concentration is higher in closed spaces, crowded rooms, and city subways. In caves and at the bottom of some wells it can be high enough to be lethal. (It *was* lethal in the Black Hole of Calcutta, where one hundred and forty-six prisoners were left in a room 18 ft. by 14 ft. by 6 ft. with one small window, on the hot night of June 20, 1756. Only twenty were found alive the next morning.)

As the prevailing winds of the earth—west to east—leave ocean areas and blow onto land areas, the carbon dioxide concentration is rather low, but it rises as it picks up the products of combustion from cities. Blowing over the ocean again it loses some carbon dioxide to the water, although on a worldwide basis this seems to be a slow process. We do know that the amount of carbon dioxide stored in the oceans in various chemical forms is about fifty times that in the air. The solubility is increased at lower temperatures, which explains why the air near the polar caps is so low in carbon dioxide.

One of the peculiarities of carbon dioxide is that it absorbs infrared or heat rays. This selective absorption can become catastrophically important to the weather and climate of the world with only a modest increase in the over-all total concentration. The reason is connected with the fact that, whereas all sunlight is to some extent converted to heat on the earth, the radiation back to space in the form of infrared rays tends to be blocked by the absorption properties of carbon dioxide. This is known as the "greenhouse effect" (more energy comes in than goes out). Thus with appreciable increases in the carbon dioxide content of the world's air, due to the enormous increase of the burning of fuels containing carbon, we face in a few decades a massive change in climate. In the first fifty years of the twentieth century the over-all increase in carbon dioxide was from 0.029 to 0.033 per cent, and since 1950 the rate of combustion of fuels has raced ahead and will continue to do so at an even faster pace as other countries catch up with the United States as fuel hogs, and as the world's population skyrockets.

This tropical-climate effect of increased carbon dioxide might be regarded as rather fun in some latitudes, except for one thing: eventually the polar ice caps will melt, the oceans will seek a new equilibrium, and the coastal cities of the world (New York, London, New Orleans, Rotterdam, etc.) will be permanently inundated.

On a truly planetary scale, this is not merely a Sunday-supplement scare story, it is an absolute certainty. It represents as sure a catastrophe on a scale of decades as does the burning-out or explosion of the sun on a scale of eons. It is perhaps unfair to man, who has only for a few decades been able to do anything important enough to the atmosphere to really matter, to suddenly accuse him of endangering the stability of the gigantic tonnage of air mass surrounding him. But this is the fact. At the present rate of increase in the burning of fuels this version of air pollution will become perhaps the number one problem of the twenty-first century. Again, with some aura of irony, it appears that nuclear fission and nuclear fusion, those master scarecrows which have frightened the naive since 1945 with their own threat of air pollution, seem to be the only way out. It is solely by converting the great and innumerable engines of our technical society to nuclear power that we can avoid the dilemma which we have created. Luckily for our great-grandchildren, it appears that the race to exhaust the fossil fuel resources of the planet (petroleum and coal) is being run at about the same pace as the race to develop nuclear power.

In the meantime, from other, more modern kinds of air pollution, as will be shown in the following chapters, we are likely to have some nasty decades ahead and some very sick people on our hands.

chapter 2

HOW IT ALL STARTED

> The suffering man ought really to consume his own
> smoke; there is no good in emitting smoke till you
> have made it into fire.
>
> CARLYLE, *"The Hero as a Man of Letters"*

In a state of nature with man not around, there is still a gentle
sort of air pollution. A great deal of poetic nonsense has been
written about country and mountain air but the truth is that,
until one gets above the timber line, the air of well vegetated
mountain and hills is miasmic with the exudation of plants. This
is a very complex perfumed mess, but there are some curious
regularities about it. On the banks of streams, when the ecolog-
ical equilibrium between plants struggling for favorable locations is established, each stream and in fact each length or curl
of a stream may be redolent of its own private blend of essential oils, depending on the plants that have established themselves on the banks.

This is the accepted explanation of why homing fish like
salmon are able to return to spawn in the precise pool they were
themselves spawned in. The water is infused continually with
a blend of plant oils peculiar to that spot and the salmon's
delicate sense of taste can identify it as home base, even after
his two-year adventure on the salty high seas.

It appears that early man was somewhat fearful, and perhaps
justifiably so, of rank vegetation. There seems to be evidence
that hay fever and other allergic diseases caused by plant pollen

or plant exudation of one kind or another were even more of a nuisance to early man than they are to us. It is believed that ancient man was not favorably impressed with the smell of flowers and in fact suspected all such odors, until the revolutionary development of perfumes by the Egyptians. (It is known, incidentally, that certain fading orchids emit ethylene gas—a smog component that can damage other plants.)

In ancient literature there is constant reference to "miasmas." Some of these involved rank vegetation and marshes but there was probably some connection in man's mind with subterranean things. Occasionally, of course, volcanic eruptions scared and in some cases poisoned him by air pollution. Fluorosis or fluorine poisoning has been noted in human bones in Iceland caused by volcanic eruptions thousands of years ago. The suffocation of Pliny the Elder by volcanic fumes is described by Tacitus. In the case of natural gas leaks, Mesopotamian man seems to have regarded these with a sort of reverent horror, although the Babylonians were not too overawed to make prudent use of natural asphalt, and in fact to make it the basis of a profitable building industry.

The town of Hit, about 100 miles west of Babylon, was the center of asphalt mining, and here were located many fissures in the rocks, exhaling natural gas. King Tukulti, a sophisticated Egyptian, visited there in 900 B.C. and tells of camping at a place "where the voice of the gods issueth from the ulmeta rocks." The Sumerians conceived of the habitable earth as floating on a large lake, the domain of the gods, from which rivers and wells received their water. Asphalt bitumen, oozing out along with water, was naturally associated with the underworld. It was believed to be the symbol of the powerful evil spirits whence it came rising to harm mankind. The Bible speaks of "the lake of pitch which is Hell."

THE BREATH OF LIFE

Middle-East asphalt is very high in sulfur, and the odors of hot sulfurous gases is undoubtedly one of the most unpleasant known to man. It is not hard to see how brimstone became associated with Hell, and that the odor of Hell is essentially the odor of the early Babylonian smog produced in the town of Hit, where the asphalt-melters plied their trade.

In fact, going far back from Babylon, man-made air pollution first really arrived with the discovery of fire management. It is believed that man probably was a carrier of fire (snatching burning branches from lightning-caused forest and brush fires) and a preserver of fire before he found out how to make it by wood friction or stone percussion. There are still natives (the Andamanese) who don't know, or probably more likely have forgotten, how to make fire but still know how to preserve it. South American natives maintain fires indefinitely on piles of earth in canoes.

It is considered likely that early man used fire for purposes other than cooking or heating. Quite likely he first used fire for scaring other creatures, including other men; for primitive religious purposes, and out of sheer mischief. There was a certain amount of goatishness in man from the start.

In the long millennia before written records, there was one positively astounding discovery in fire-making which seems to have been made early in Southeastern Asia and to have spread through the Malay peninsula and to the Philippines but never to have reached populations greatly more sophisticated in other ways, such as the early Egyptians and Chinese. This was the "fire-pump." It is based on the incredibly advanced idea that air is heated when it is rapidly pumped ("adiabatically compressed" in scientific language), and that one can start a fire, therefore, by closely fitting a wooden cylinder and piston together, placing tinder in a groove in the piston, pounding on the piston, and then quickly withdrawing it with the tinder aflame. That such a device should have been invented in prehistoric Southeastern Asia is almost as unbelievable as if an early Eskimo had invented the diesel engine, and in fact the principle is identical to that of the diesel engine.

The forgotten Malaysian who conceived this complicated notion must have possessed a genius more overpowering than that of Leonardo da Vinci, since rubbed sticks and flint sparks were essentially still being used in historical communities to light fires until the time of the phosphorous match in 1827. Anthropologists regard the fire-pump as an inexplicable miracle in man's intellectual history. One can go further and truly state that man had created his first smog from an internal combustion engine in the operation of this gadget, which remains mysteriously outside the context of human development.

As man became cleverer at managing fire, he became an expert on natural fuels. When wood was hard to come by, bones were often used. Dried dung became popular. Even today in India cattle dung is so important as fuel that its value as manure is neglected. When neither wood nor dung were available, animal oils and fats were used. These gave smooth, stable flames and very little carbon monoxide; otherwise the Eskimos would never have survived. In some circumstances complete animals were used for fuels. Examples are the stormy petrel and the candlefish which, being extremely rich in fat, burn heartily without a wick.

Tinder, as a means of getting the wood fire started, was a very fussy technical business. Dried moss and especially dried fungus, the down or floss of seeds, and rotten dry wood were carefully collected and stored. Of necessity, early man found out which woods would burn according to his specifications. As everyone knows who has had his try at amateur woodcraft, making a fire without matches usually ends up in a mess of sweat, acrimony, and frustration, with everybody giving unwanted and ineffectual advice. Wood fires are hard to start in the damp temperate zones; moreover, very early in history man came to dislike the excessive smoke of wood fires (an old Spanish proverb states that there are only three things that will drive a man from his house: a leaky roof, a talkative wife, and smoke). Thus came quite early in history a tremendous invention in smog control—the discovery of wood charcoal. (The talkative wives are still with us.)

Charcoal was made by heaping wood faggots together to form a kind of domelike oven, then lighting a fire in the center. The wood partly burns and distills off resins and tar, leaving a handy, light, smokeless fuel. Charcoal has one serious drawback that resulted in many deaths throughout classical and medieval times. When it is burned without special precautions, it gives off carbon monoxide. Most of these deaths from carbon monoxide poisoning in the poorly ventilated hearths of houses and castles rather than in the furnaces of metallurgy and commerce seem in old times to have been attributed to excessive drinking, since it was customary through many centuries for the good folk to eat and drink themselves into a stupor before a winter evening's charcoal fire. This was a disease of the rich, however, since charcoal usually cost too much for the poor and for the most part so did alcohol.

It is extraordinary how long after man had learned of the existence and of the handiness of coal he refused to use it as a fuel. At the time of Marco Polo it was regarded as a most unnatural kind of fuel. Its sulfurous fumes revolted the medieval taste and unquestionably its behavior was again associated with the smell of brimstone and Hell.

Coal came into use because wood had become scarce in

Elizabethan England. The sudden acceptance of coal represented a noteworthy victory of the commercial instinct over aesthetics and health, since England at the time was enjoying a formidable industrial boom. Prohibition of the use, import, and transportation of coal had previously existed in England, Germany, and other European countries. During the reign of Edward I (1272–1307) there was recorded a protest by the nobility against the use of "sea" coal, and in the suceeding reign of Edward II a man was put to torture for filling the air with a "pestilential odor," through the burning of coal. Under Richard II and later under Henry V, England regulated coal because of smoke and odors. Taxation rather than torture or execution was applied for the first time. Henry V established a commission to oversee the movement of coal into the City of London.

But with the reign of the first Elizabeth, the dam burst, and London promptly all but drowned in coal smoke. Industrial activity was skyrocketing. Between 1580, when Shakespeare is supposed to have settled in London, and the Restoration in 1660, imports of goods in London increased by a factor of twenty-five. Foreigners traveling to Elizabethan London were astonished and revolted at the filthy smoke from tens of thousands of domestic fires and workshops. They had seen no spectacle like it on earth. Breweries, soap and starch houses, brick kilns, sugar refineries, etc., were pouring out smoke. London seemed unfit for human habitation. By the Restoration Great Britain was producing some 2 million tons of coal per year, about five times more than all the rest of the world.

Typically of the English, it seems to have been the nasty taste of beer that caused the most annoyance. Coal-burning was used in the drying of malt and, just as peat smoke is known to impart the familiar expensive flavor to Scotch, coal smoke gave English beer a nauseating bouquet which was compared to "the taste of vile ordure of Hogges." Even the hardiest tipplers could hardly stand this brew. The first unsuccessful large-scale attempts were made about this time to make coke out of coal, analogous to producing charcoal from wood. It was in Derbyshire that a solution was found to the beer problem. About the time of the English Civil War (1642–48) some enterprising maltsters brewed beer from malt dried with "coaks" made from a special kind of hard coal dug near Derby. This beer was found to be sweet and pure, and Derbyshire beer became famous.

We have no reports on the effects of the Elizabethan deluge of smog on public health, but from what we know of more recent disasters in London (see next chapter), the classical combination of coal smoke with fog must have taken its toll. However, the mercantile English were reluctant to take any steps that would endanger their coal-based economy, and since London smogs killed mostly older, poorer people, who didn't expect to live very long anyway in those days, comfort was taken in excessive alcoholic consumption. With the development of cheap gin, the early eighteenth century in London saw perhaps the most colossal example of universal public alcoholism in history before or since, and minor causes of public unhealthiness, such as polluted air, went unnoticed. (It is even possible that with the everpresent odor of juniper berries and alcohol, the exhalation from rotting teeth, and sour bowels, the average poor Londoner would hardly have noticed the smell of sulfur dioxide and of industrial aerosols floating about.)

The nobility and intelligentsia, however, occasionally became critical and even constructive. John Evelyn, a noted busybody and do-gooder and one of the founding members of the Royal Society, wrote a pamphlet in 1661, which was ordered to be published by Charles II, "Furnifogium, or the Inconvenience of Air and Smoke of London Dissapated; together with Some Remedies Humbly Proposed." In 1686 Justel presented before the Philosophical Society "An account of an Engine that Consumes Smoke." The suggestions made were lively and imaginative rather than practicable, but it is worth pointing out that Justel's smoke-consuming monster embodies a concept that has recently been emphasized by Professor Fritz Zwicky of Cal Tech.

It must be emphasized that up until now the main concern with air pollution had been with the odors rather than the hygiene of polluted air. As we have seen, this was true even in the case of asphaltic bitumen, and the early resistance to coal as a fuel. It is true to a large extent even now, although grievances about eye-irritation have been added. Since the smell of pollution is socially so important, we will review briefly the subject of odor.

Man is regarded as a rank amateur in smelling, perhaps unjustifiably so, because he is compared with some of his mammalian companions, such as the dog, who is a master at smelling. About $\frac{1}{20}$th of the human brain consists of tissue concerned with smelling, whereas the proportion is about $\frac{1}{3}$ in the case of dogs. When a dog comes home from a walk, one asks him not what he saw but what he smelled. A so-called "anosmic" dog (with olfactory organs destroyed) is not only pitiful, he is useless and loses all qualities of affection and alertness. An anosmic human being (and many albinos are so afflicted from birth) is still in business. It is supposed that the ancestors of man had a better sense of smell than now, but when Homo sapiens began to stand upright and get his face away from the ground, his visual and audio organs proliferated at the expense of the olfactory.

The exterior organ of smell in man is a yellow-brown patch

high up in the nose and about the size of a dime, covered with a wet mucous membrane. Nobody knows exactly how it works. It has been vaguely concluded that it is a chemical or catalytic process in which molecules of the odorant dissolve in the membrane, set off some sort of chemical reaction, which is relayed to the olfactory bulb of the brain. A more recent theory is that the exterior organs of smell send out infrared rays which, if absorbed in a certain part of the spectrum, result in localized energy effects due to selective absorption by the odorant.

Man actually is far from being an olfactory cripple. His ability to smell musk, for example, is astonishing, even in comparison with such incredible feats as the detection by the male gypsy moth of the female seven miles upwind. Recently this female moth exudate was identified chemically as a grease-like higher alcohol with a slight leathery odor, which is unnoticed by any other insect or animal species, but the male moth can pick it up with its antennae in concentrations of less than 1 part in a quadrillion parts of air. However, this is only about eight times as sensitive as the response of the human nose to musk.

The human sense of smell is rather temperamental. For instance, it tires easily. When the olfactory mucous membrane becomes fatigued, the ability to distinguish different odors disappears according to a different sequence; and after recuperation returns in the same sequence. When one can no longer smell tincture of iodine, the odor of turpentine is still perceptible and the smell of lavender remains quite strong. When the ability to smell returns after a cold, one can smell oil of cloves before the odor of a roast cooking, and both of these precede the ability to smell rubber.

Old medical practitioners of the Osler school could "smell"

diseases. The doctor would visit the house, tell the mother not to wake the child, open the bedroom door quietly, sniff and say "scarlet fever." As we all know, nothing can exceed the sensitivity of a woman's nose for alcohol on her husband's breath or for tobacco in her young son's clothes. There have been some famous smellers in history, including Turgeniev, Huysman, Baudelaire, and especially Zola. Zola's nose was so sensitive that he was examined by a panel of medical experts, in the interest of science. It is ironical that Zola and his wife were killed by carbon monoxide from a defective stove.

Early man's sense of smell can be assumed to have been based on evolutionary selection. There was no reason in man's early development for his nose to recognize carbon monoxide with alarm, since it was not a part of his million years of environment, hence regrettably it remains odorless to us today. On the other hand, man reacts with commendable sharpness to ethyl mercaptan (skunk odor) as do all mammals and even snakes. (Snakes incidentally are repelled by man's odor, which is the reason rattlesnakes will not crawl across a cowboy's lariat; they are revolted, not by rope fuzz, as it is often erroneously suggested, but by the odor of sweat from human hands.) The toxic hydrogen sulfide, probably on account of early volcanic sources and to some extent on account of the gases from human feces and other dangerously unedible substances, is well perceived by man.

The odor of flowers was no more pleasant to early man than to a cow whose sense of smell leads her to choose certain weeds to eat and certain to avoid. (Albino rhinoceroses and sheep, having defective smell sense, often die from eating poisonous grasses.)

In early Egyptian times incense and perfume were invented

and originally this seems to have been associated with religious rites. (From a practical standpoint, incense possibly was burned to neutralize the smells of ancient temples, since the casual toilet habits of the Egyptians and Mesopotamians rendered them otherwise rather gamy.) The ancient Egyptian word for smell referring to perfume is always combined in a form equivalent to "fragrance of the gods." Perfume was used to make the worshiper acceptable to the gods rather than to other human beings, since the gods were presumed to be especially pleased by perfumes.

Since the animal sources of later European man's powerful perfumes, such as the musk deer, the whale's ambergris, the civet and the beaver, were not available to the Near East cultures, the perfumes were made usually by *enfleurage* (soaking of flower petals in animal oils or greases) or maceration, using kitchen tools to filter off the herb residues. Popular essences were calamus, cassia, cinnamon, sandalwood, rosemary, peppermint, heliotrope, rushes, and ginger. The psalmist speaks of "the precious ointment upon the head, but ran down upon the beard, even Aaron's beard: that went down the skirts of his garments" (Ps. CXXXIII 2). Bells or cones of pomade can be seen in pictures of Egyptian life on the heads of guests at early Egyptian festivities.

The transference of perfumery and indeed of the sense of smell itself from religious rites to purely human relationships must, however, have been fairly early in racial history. People smelled one another rather than kissing. In Sanskrit the word for kissing, *ghra,* means smell. In ancient Persia the word for "love" means smell. In classical Greek there was no word kiss, and in the Maori language there is no expression for "I greet you" except the phrase "I smell you." Maoris are among those who use the "nose kiss" and, as we know, oriental societies were profoundly revolted when first exposed to Western kissing behavior.

It appears that pleasure in smelling increases with its uselessness, so that smelling as an aesthetic act, aside from sex and religion, is relatively a novelty for man and emerges only when cultures have leisure enough to evolve poetry and other luxurious recreations.

In relation to sex, it is often overlooked that this is not always a one-way street, with the male eternally chasing after natural or artificial perfumes given off by the female. It has been found recently that female mice show adjustments of their sexual cycle when they detect the odor of males of their own species. Recently mated female mice will fail to become pregnant if they are subjected to the smell of strange males. Women detect the odor from a mixture of cholesterol with testasterone acetate (male hormone) at much lower concentrations than do men. These rather delicate differentiations might have become more important in a society in which men didn't produce so many overwhelming smells, mostly of a foul nature. In effect, the odor of personal and social smog has obscured what could have been as exquisite and essential a biological relation as that between worker bees and their queen.

Man in fact has often indulged, as Nietzsche says, in "the delight to stink." The early kings of France were inordinately proud of the strong smell of their armpits. In Zola's *La Terre* and of course in Rabelais whole chapters are given over to descriptions of feats of outstanding prowess in the art of breaking wind. All this has been updated, incidentally, by Lawrence Durrell, whose literary powers, at least in reference to cloacal events, are unmatched.

The production of displeasing smells has throughout history been accompanied by rather pathetic countermeasures, especially on the part of women. One recalls the old wives' use of a strand of burning cotton string hung on the kitchen door knob to neutralize the smell of cooking cabbage and frying fish. The wholly unscientific use of chlorophyll preparations for absorbing disagreeable domestic odors has been sold to American housewives over the past few decades in perhaps one of the most egregious commercial con-games ever perpetrated. It is unnecessary to point out that perfume itself has for centuries been used as a maskant for underlying filthy smells rather than solely for the further embellishment of well-scrubbed bodies. In the court of Louis XIV the nostalgic memoirs of the courtiers mention the haunting bouquet resulting from the fact that those who were kept waiting too long for their audience had to retire suddenly behind the palace drapes to move their bowels and doused themselves with perfume upon re-emergence. In modern days this pathos is matched by numerous proposals such as the notion of adding perfume to diesel fuels so that the acrid odor of formaldehyde in the exhaust smoke will be gentled over by some automotive equivalent of Chanel No. 5. We will discuss such curious expedients in a later chapter.

One aspect of odors on a social basis merits brief consideration. Do various human races have peculiar odors repugnant to other races?

It has been reported, for example, that to the American Indians the white settlers stank. It is noteworthy, however, that these complaints ceased when Indians began to wear clothes and adopt the white man's other habits. The Navajo Indians do have a somewhat generalized stench which has been rationally explained by such anthropologists as La Farge as being due to the wood smoke in their ill-ventilated hogans. White men who decide to live in hogans come up with the same aroma.

Some African natives smell bad to us, because of the rancid

oil or butter with which they smear their bodies to repel insects. However, the notion that there is a peculiar African (or Afro-American) body odor, which fits in gracefully with policies of racial segregation, is imbecilic nonsense.

chapter **3**

THE DISASTERS

Hell is a city much like London—a populous and
smoky city.

SHELLEY, *Peter Bell the Third*

When air pollution is sudden and serious enough so that a
lot of people die in a hurry, this is a disaster. We know this,
because the newspapers run the story on the first page and the
"continued on page 11" runovers are labeled "Smog Disaster."
However, people are pretty hard to kill overnight with dirty
air, so the immediate death statistics are seldom very terrifying.
It is much easier to slay people spectacularly with earthquakes
or in airplane or automobile crashes. Indeed, the true extent
of an air pollution disaster is not even suspected until much
later, when the "excess deaths" in a community are analyzed
by medical statisticians. Even this figure, which indicates the
number of people in a community who probably died later as
the result of heart disease and delayed pulmonary complications
caused by the air-pollution event, is not very edifying, unless
the community is normally used to pure air. What does "excess
deaths" mean in chronically polluted cities such as London,
Los Angeles and Tokyo?

Most of the isolated catastrophes have involved industrial
accidents coupled with an unusual degree of temporary
temperature inversion. (Temperature inversion means that the
upper layers of air become hotter, rather than, as is normally
the case, cooler than ground air. Since air normally circulates

by going from hotter to colder spots, temperature inversion prevents vertical circulation and keeps the foul air on the ground at breathing level.) Typical cases of sudden inversion are those of the Meuse Valley and Donora.

The Meuse Valley in Belgium contains a large number of industrial plants that before World War II steadily gave off some mildly toxic amounts of gases such as sulfur dioxide and hydrofluoric acid. Suddenly, in the five days of December 1 to December 5, 1930, temperature inversion caught up with the Meuse Valley, and sixty people died. It was a rather pitiful case of industrial and rural communities being suddenly drowned together in poisonous air. It was not as unexpected as it seemed at the time, since the history of the Meuse Valley peasants and their animals had been a rather shaky one, ever since sulfuric acid plants were introduced into the vicinity. In 1897 at Huy, further up the valley than the 1930 disaster, a poisonous fog lasted three days. The peasants found that they could protect themselves to some extent by breathing through handkerchiefs and they even provided cloth nose-bags for their cattle. A so-called "fog asthma" afflicted cattle in 1902 and again in 1911.

In 1930, however, there was curiously little expert diagnosis of the incident. (Perhaps in 1930 people expected all manner of afflictions.) The inversion that year was so unexpected that panicky stories of mysterious and unindentified poisonous gas were still being carried by the newspapers many months after the misfortune. A popular Sunday-supplement story at this time was the one about the "pogonip," a deathly fog that was supposed to descend on lonely innocent valleys in the Rocky Mountains and to leave the victims desolated, as if by strychnine in their whiskey. Modern smogsters in retrospect believe that sulfur dioxide in the form of "aerosols" (fine mist-like water particles in which the sulfur dioxide can be converted to sulfuric acid) possibly in evil combination with small amounts of hydrofluoric acid caused the Meuse Valley deaths. The aerosols are standard air contaminants wherever sulfur is burned, either in high-sulfur fuel or in industrial chemical operations, but there has to be free water in the air. It was the inversion that suddenly kept this wet, sour mess at ground level and rubbed the peoples' and the animals' noses in it. Inversion was the real villain, as we will find to be true in nearly all cases of pollution accidents.

The real shock of the Meuse Valley lay in the realization that temperature inversions can take place where they are not anticipated. A community, therefore, must live as if it expected judgment day tomorrow, since inversion may turn all its sloppy little sins suddenly into mortal ones. Cities such as Denver, proud of its high sparkling air, rather expected smog to be chronic in great lewd, low-lying metropolises such as London and Los Angeles, but found not long ago to its shame and dismay that inversion was also possible a mile high in the Rockies, and that the mountain people could suffer the pangs of smog as acutely as the inhabitants of the sea-level Gomorrahs.

Donora, Pennsylvania, was hit by fog and temperature inversion on October 26, 1948. This town was located on the inside on the horseshoe-shaped Monongahela River valley, and when the inversion hit, all the fumes from a steel factory, a sulfuric acid plant, and a zinc plant were bottled up in the town. The sulfur dioxide concentration reached 2 parts per million, forty-three per cent of the population was made ill, and twenty persons died, mostly on the third day. Mainly old men were the victims. An old man would find himself coughing, the cough would become a bitter paroxysm, he would sit down on the curb and totter over dead.

The Donora and the Meuse Valley episodes were very much alike. It is agreed that sulfuric aerosols were again the poisons but they represented normal pollution suddenly made deadly by inversion and fog.

Poza Rica near Mexico City on November 23–24, 1950 was something else again. A petroleum plant was located here in which sulfur was recovered from natural gas. Somebody made a mistake and a whole tank full of hydrogen sulfide (the most toxic of the sulfurous gases) was released to the atmosphere. Twenty-two people died almost immediately and 320 were hospitalized. Hydrogen sulfide hits fast. Gaugers, walking on the top of great tanks of "sour crude" (containing hydrogen sulfide), have been known to be overcome so suddenly that they fell off the tanks and broke their necks. One of the silly and dangerous things that teenaged chemical students are often allowed to do is to generate hydrogen sulfide by reacting metal sulfides with strong acids. This compound has such a sickening rotten-egg odor that it is erroneously believed that, just as in the case of ammonia, the violent smell will keep the student from breathing injurious amounts. Unfortunately, this has been shown not to be the case, since people vary greatly in their tolerance to the smell, but not in their tolerance to the poison; it kills everybody fast.

The slow-killing smogs of Great Britain again involve the aerosols, since it is the combination of sulfur dioxide from coal smoke and fog that is the murderer, as in the Meuse Valley and at Donora. The term "smog" (smoke + fog) was invented before World War I and probably grew out of Des Voeux's 1911 report to the Manchester Conference of the Smoke Abatement League on the "smoke-fog" deaths which occurred in Scotland in 1909 (1063 deaths were claimed to have been caused by smog in Glasgow and Edinburgh that year). This is the only correct use of the term "smog." As will be explained later, the Los Angeles situation mistakenly referred to as smog involves neither smoke nor fog.

The English and Scottish cities had long suffered this condition, but London was the worst, since fog and temperature inversion are somewhat more common there. In the previous chapter we have seen that peoples' lives were unquestionably being taken as early as the reign of the first Elizabeth, when England began to use coal in quantity. Since that time until now the lungs of London dwellers have been black. An English medical student, working on corpses, so rarely sees a nice pink lung that when he does he probably concludes the deceased was an Irishman. However, deaths directly attributed to soot alone (aside from cancer lesions, which are another story) are rare, and it has only been prolonged fog along with temperature inversion preventing the dissipation of sulfur dioxide that have caused such an obvious increase in death rate that scandal resulted.

Some such prolonged smog in London seems to have killed several thousand people in 1872, but nothing much was done about it, except to set up smoke-abatement committees, which abated no smoke. Only a vague idea then existed in regard to the role of sulfurous aerosols. When smoke by itself, without sulfur dioxide and fog, had been found to be fairly innocuous, the smoke-abatement programs lost their sense of urgency. It was also observed that fog, without smoke and sulfurous aerosols, is harmless, although the accidental occurrence of flu epidemics with periods of stubborn fogs in London had confused the medical authorities (a prolonged fog in London in 1958, without the other ingredients, had no demonstratable effect).

In recent years things came to a head in London with the "Black Fog" of December 5–9, 1952, which brought the city to a standstill and caused 4000 deaths in four days. This is perhaps the most serious air-pollution disaster in history, probably taking more lives than the Second Battle of Ypres in which chlorine gas was first used in World War I. The 4000 casualties still remains a guess, since the number of "excess deaths" remained high in London for several months. Deaths were due mostly to heart failure associated with acute respiratory distress, but the incidence of "chronic bronchitis," "emphysema," etc., in London has been high for so long that the excess death statistics probably mean little.

The unforgettable "Black Fog" started out on Thursday morning, December 4, 1952 as a white fog, and looked to be simply another pea-souper or "London particular." It was thicker than usual, but its extraordinary denseness caused gaiety rather than panic—the sort of dogged mass exhilaration that this greatest and bravest of all cities had learned to develop even during the wartime blitzes. Buses proceeded at two miles per hour, with the conductor walking out in front, guiding the driver. Cars went in pokey convoys of ten to twenty. A big duck flying blind crashed through the roof of Victoria Station and fell at the feet of waiting passengers. At a greyhound track that night the dogs lost sight of the rabbit and the race had to be postponed. One dog got lost altogether and was found a half hour later sniffing for the rabbit in the bookies' tent. At Sadler's Wells they got through the first act of La Traviata before so much fog seeped into the theater that the singers could no longer see the conductor. At the movies only the spectators in the first four rows could see the screen.

At London airport, one pilot after landing with instruments got lost trying to taxi to the passenger terminal. A search party went out, but it got lost too. An Air France plane was marooned for two hours away from the terminal and during this time the passengers drank up all the champagne and brandy on board. People resorted to the subways, and one couple emerging at their station, confused as to which direction to take to their home, was accosted by a mysterious figure from the fog who inquired their address and guided them directly to it. When they asked him how he got his bearings so well, he replied "I'm blind." On Friday transportation was so impossible that working men went to police stations to spend the night. Members of Parliament were issued blankets and bunked down in the lounges of the House. Firemen answering calls walked ahead of their engines. Police patrolled the docks in lifejackets, but even so scores of people drowned simply from stepping into the river.

By Friday the fog had changed from white to brown and by Saturday morning it was black, the gaiety had gone. Now people began to die very fast. By Saturday noon all the doctors in London were on the run and all the hospitals were full. Because of lack of mobility, many doctors spent hours at a time at their telephones, desperately advising their patients to get to an oxygen tent, somehow, somewhere. By Sunday morning, the visibility was eleven inches. You quite literally could not see your hand in front of your face. It was cold now, and old people lost in the smog were dying of exposure as well as acute respiratory attacks. Fifty bodies were brought in to a mortuary from one small park in South London. The smog lifted Sunday afternoon.

It is perhaps typically British that a more careful study of the deaths of animals than of human beings during the Black Fog was carried out. The Smithfield Cattle Show was taking place when the smog hit. The prize bovines suffered badly but sheep and pigs were not affected. Fat on the show cattle increased their susceptibility to cardio-respiratory failure. The relatively lean ones survived. Another striking observation was that the show animals who had dirty pens survived, while those in scrupulously clean quarters died. The explanation is believed to be that ammonia and urea from the uncleaned pens acted as neutralizers for the sulfurous aerosols. It has been deduced that, during a bad London smog, mothers should not change their babies' diapers too often.

Cattle were also killed during the Meuse Valley episode but do not seem to have suffered in Donora, nor did horses and dogs, although canaries were seriously affected. All the canaries in Poza Rica were killed, which is to be expected, since hydrogen sulfide acts through the bloodstream and birds are much more sensitive to this form of poisoning, including carbon monoxide, for which they have been used as indicators.

The London block-buster smogs will continue from time to time as long as the English burn soft coal in any appreciable amount. In fact, what looked to be the start of a very serious smog took place in December, 1962. Smoke concentration reached 10 times normal, with sulfur dioxide content 14 times normal, within 24 hours. The situation was saved by the slow rise of the warm-air ceiling of the inversion, which gave the smog room to dilute itself. Finally the winds changed and the smog was blown out to sea.

As the danger passed, British health authorities were inclined to celebrate. They considered that the control methods set into motion after the Clean Air Act of 1958 had saved London from another disaster. At least they had eliminated a good deal of the smoke in the fatal trio of sulfur dioxide, smoke, and fog. Of the 486 smoke-control areas, a quarter are now listed as smoke-free. Dark smoke from any chimney, domestic or industrial, is an offense in these areas. Otherwise, say the authorities, 1962's smog would have been worse than 1952's, since there is much more coal being burned today.

Admittedly the control measures have not routed the sulfurous aerosols, which can still form when the windless, foggy inversion takes place. Devices to control an excess of sulfur dioxide in the air are very costly and actually would require an overnight revolution in fuel habits, which England is not willing to consider. Simply substituting petroleum for coal would not do the job, since the available fuel oil from the Middle East is also high in sulfur. Even substituting natural gas for coal or petroleum would not entirely solve the problem, since with a swarming automobile population London smogs would ultimately become "smogs" of the Los Angeles type, where sulfur aerosols are only a minor poison, and the people have other, weirder pollutants to worry about.

In fact, London has been lucky. Its serious inversions during the winters have been few. It is not even as smoky year in and year out as Manchester, where Londoners claim the people are waked up early every morning by the sounds of birds coughing.

The British hate to give up burning things. Nothing stirs as much nostalgia in the British as the picture of a little home with a plume of smoke snaking out of a chimney. Of course this should be a chimney in a cottage in Kent, but now we must realize that these little symbols of White Christmases that reside in the Saxon heart, whether they be referring to Kent, Heidelberg, or Mamaroneck, are skull-and-crossbones symbols. They should be associated, not with Christmas music, but with the buzz of rattlesnakes.

chapter 4

THE RED-FACED STIFFS

... the proficient poison of sure sleep ...
E. E. CUMMINGS, *When the Proficient
Poison of Sure Sleep*

In any discussion of air pollution, carbon monoxide must be wound like a shroud around the proceedings. We have referred rather casually to its debut into the life of mankind. It entered with fire. When man invented charcoal, carbon monoxide glided into both the home and the work-place. When man invented the blast furnace it swirled over heavy industry, and when man invented the automobile, it was produced and took its pale refuge in all the streets and all the tunnels of the world.

"CO" (see-oh, as all chemists pronounce it) is thus a pure creation of man in the latest millennia of his life on earth. If it had been part of the very early environment of man—if it had been as constantly his companion as staphylococcus bacteria, for example, man's evolving body probably would have found a defense against it or at least a way for his senses to recognize it and cry alarm.

One of the striking things about CO is the dreadful simplicity with which it kills. Nothing could be easier than the mechanism of this way of death.

Oxygen is carried through the bodies of mammals by attaching itself to hemoglobin in the blood. The hemoglobin molecule, which contains iron, picks up oxygen in a loose complex, becoming much redder in color, and by way of the arteries visits all

[51]

of the body. After the hemoglobin has released its load of oxygen to the brain and the liver and all the other organs and tissues, it returns, now a paler color, through the vein system to the lungs, to get more oxygen.

What if the hemoglobin, coming back to the lungs, now meets with CO as well as oxygen? There occurs an act of sheer piracy. The CO takes over the hemoglobin, brushing the oxygen aside. Carbon monoxide has an affinity for the hemoglobin (forming carboxyl-hemoglobin) roughly two hundred and ten times as strong as oxygen's affinity. Hence it is a matter of brutal mathematics to estimate how much CO has to be in the lung to capture virtually all of the hemoglobin. Each little hemoglobin skiff then becomes a much brighter red than with oxygen and sails back through the arterial blood with its new cargo.

This cargo is not wanted. It is not that the CO, complexed as carboxyl-hemoglobin, wounds or poisons the oxygen-thirsty tissues, it is simply that these tissues do not know what to do with the CO. They are expecting oxygen and they get something they have never been taught to deal with. They can't use CO in their business of cell chemistry, which is the business of living. The hemoglobin sails right on through, with its cargo undelivered, and then makes its way back through the vein system unchanged. (In a body poisoned with CO not only do the face and neck and extremities become blushfully red, because carboxyl-hemoglobin is so red, but the venous blood is as bright as the arterial blood—a shocking reversal of nature which was noted by seventeenth-century medicos before the existence of any such thing as carbon monoxide was suspected.)

This business of undelivered cargoes and CO-dominated hemoglobin cannot go on very long, since some of the organs, especially the brain, begin to get into very bad trouble without their accustomed oxygen supply. The brain tissues actually begin to make ammonia, which can be smelled in post mortem examination, and are on their way to being irreversibly damaged. At this point there is only one desperate act that could save the victim, and it is rather strange that this has been realized only recently: he can be saved if he is put immediately in a high-pressure oxygen cell.

The reason why this works is that at high enough pressures the oxygen will dissolve in the *plasma* of the blood, skipping the elaborate mechanism of hemoglobin transportation and will thus be immediately circulated to the oxygen-starved tissues, especially to the weakling brain. It has been found that mice can live in an atmosphere containing ridiculously high concentrations of CO, providing that the air is at high enough pressure so that oxygen can dissolve in the watery plasma.

The simplicity of carbon monoxide's attack on the body leads one to wonder what form a few hundred thousand years of additional evolution might take to protect the body against a hypothetical steady increase in CO content of the atmosphere. Probably it would be the development of a new blood pigment, one more fastidious and selective than hemoglobin, which would reject CO molecules when it encounters them in the lung. However, it might be something more radical such as the development of an ability on the part of the body tissues to use CO as a substitute for oxygen. Recent studies have shown that animal tissues, kept alive in a bath of synthetic blood, can be taught to use a little bit of CO instead of oxygen for some of their problems in cell chemistry.

Carbon monoxide is colorless and odorless—almost. At extremely high concentrations, far above the toxic threshold, it has a faint not unpleasing garlic odor. The organs of dead victims of acute CO poisoning under autopsy exude unmistakably the garlic smell, since the concentration process in the blood of the corpse has been a very powerful one; in fact it is the envy of chemical engineers who for their own purposes might want to obtain CO in purified form, since it is a versatile compound used in many important industrial chemical processes.

The fact that CO poisoning seems essentially to be a process of suffocation (oxygen starvation) rather than some spectacular chemical corrosion of the vital tissues has led to oversimplification on the part of American hygienists. It is easy to see why. If it is simply suffocation, then the same symptoms and prognosis should generally apply as in the case of a child who locks himself in a junk-yard refrigerator. This is proving not to be the case, and the emerging facts are immensely irritating to that kind of doctor or toxicologist who likes black and white and bad men and cowboys. This is a very dangerous kind of hygienist and unfortunately, as we shall see later, he is fond of editing vast "authoritative" textbooks on the subject of toxic gases.

During the period of early industrialization, as in the England we have described, carbon monoxide was not known as such, but in 1716 the German chemist Friedrich Hoffman blamed the vapors from burning charcoal for a death that occurred in an accident in Jena. Because CO itself can be made to burn, the early chemists confused it with hydrogen. In manufactured city gas or "illuminating gas" carbon monoxide has long been a substantial component, but in countries such as the United States with large reserves of natural gas (methane), there is no longer so much CO in the mains that feed the home, hence it is less efficient nowadays to commit suicide by sticking one's head in the oven; gulping exhaust from one's automobile does a better job.

Defective hot-water heaters and gas stoves can still put out enough CO to kill a whole family in its sleep, even when they burn natural gas, and it is important to realize why this is so.

[54]

A multi-jet burner, for example, when turned low, may burn the gas jets completely to carbon *di*oxide and water only in a certain percentage of the burner orifices. Partly plugged holes may emit gas which at lower than flame temperatures is burned to CO and various other things. All burners should have a flue to channel the burnt gas out of the house, but this is a far from universal or even common practice the world over.

The situation with automobiles is roughly similar. Although ideally the gasoline should be burned to carbon dioxide and water, this is the case only in imaginary and perhaps absolutely unachievable engines. For example, an ordinary car operates with smoothest results actually when it is fed a mixture of air and fuel slightly on the rich side—that is, with more fuel than the air can completely burn to carbon dioxide and water. (This is not the case with diesel engines, which operate with large excesses of air.) Under conditions of stop-and-go city driving, idling, acceleration, deceleration, the percentage of CO in the exhaust gas may be higher than in high-speed driving. This does not mean that if all city streets are freeways with cars whizzing through them, unimpeded, the carbon monoxide in the air decreases, since at high, steady speeds the CO is produced in greater total amount, although in lower percentage of the exhaust gas. Thus at least a small amount of CO is produced under any imaginable way of running an automobile engine. On an average a thousand cars will produce about three tons of CO in the atmosphere every day.

This CO is quickly mixed with the air mainly because it is hot and is the same density as air, and hence only if you are running your car in a closed garage or are breathing through a rubber tube connected with the tail pipe are you necessarily in for a fast and painless extinction.

Some things can go badly wrong, however. Exhaust pipes

and manifolds with holes in them, for example. Or a muffler too loosely connected. CO then can seep up through the floorboard. We will never know how many fatal accidents have been caused by preliminary CO-dopiness of drivers to the point of helplessness or even coma, since there has been no systematic attempt to determine by autopsy the incidence of carboxyl-hemoglobin in the blood of the victims. There are just enough proven cases where the corpses removed from wrecks were cherry red in the face and otherwise undamaged to indicate that traffic deaths directly or indirectly caused by carbon monoxide may exceed the number of traffic deaths caused by drunkenness. CO-poisoning and intoxication by alcohol have in fact often been confused on hasty diagnosis by the highway police, since a person in the medium stages of CO intoxication may talk silly, his eyes may fail to track, and he will be very likely to stagger when he gets out of the car.

Damaged exhaust pipes or mufflers are naturally more often associated with old cars, but the wise head of a family, embarking on a long trip with any car, will have his exhaust system checked by the "hiss" or "smoke" tests (garage mechanics partly plug the tail pipe and start the engine, the leak being located by a hiss, or they put a little oil in the carburetor and notice where the smoke comes out). CO from exhaust leaks is especially likely to overcome children and more so when they are playing on the floor of the car. However, babies asleep are easy to kill with CO, and the all too frequent experiences of headachey young couples stopping at a service station to warm the bottle and finding the baby red-faced and dead are not pleasant to think about.

Salesmen who drive every day, especially under winter conditions, sometimes develop accident-proneness; this has been checked back to CO leakage. The brain, as we have noted, is the first organ to be affected by CO. There is loss of judgment and, even if the driver suspects what is wrong with him, he finds himself unable to do anything prudent about it. Looking at his wrist watch, he is unable to tell the time; it doesn't register. He cannot add up the simplest figures in his mind (the clinical term is *acalculia*). His scope of vision becomes limited, and he is unlikely to see a car barging in from a side road. He is likely to start driving on the wrong side of the highway, and in the city he is apt to bump into other cars from behind.

Young people face special hazards. During cold weather it is not unusual for a boy and girl to park the car in some Lovers' Lane or Lookout Point and because of the cold to keep the engine running at idle in order to benefit from the car heater. The police or campus monitors who may be stationed in such areas are all too familiar with the cyanotic dead bodies that have to be disentwined before further processing.

An open window in a car does not necessarily mean safety. The reason is one of aerodynamics: air flowing past the window creates a slight under-pressure in the car which tends to suck up exhaust fumes through the floor board. The front vents should be open in ordinary driving but should be shut when following close to another car in heavy traffic.

The first sign of distress from carbon monoxide is likely to be a sudden tightening across the forehead, followed by headache and throbbing in the temples. The next phase includes nausea, dimness of vision and extreme dizziness. The end is sometimes preceded by convulsions but this stage lapses into coma, depressed heart action, finally death. People who have been saved at the last moment by resuscitation are not likely ever to be normal again, if unconsciousness for any appreciable length of time has been one of the stages of the attack, since the brain tissues by then usually have been irreparably affected. The higher (cerebral) brain cannot endure more than about eight minutes of oxygen deprivation without permanent harm. The patient has a poor memory, and is inclined to become a nuisance because of extreme preoccupation with his afflictions. Among many physical after-effects one of the most sorrowful is atrophy of the hands.

The after-effects of acute but not fatal CO poisoning unfortunately are easy to confuse with the symptoms of *chronic* poisoning. Here we enter immediately into an area strangled with disputation and decorated with considerable evidence of large-scale brain-washing—at least as far as the American scene is concerned. What we are up against in arriving at the truth can be gathered from the fact that, whereas American hygienists have set 100 parts per million (p.p.m.) of CO in the atmosphere as a maximum for safety, and California has set 30 p.p.m. in smog regulations, the Russians originally set 2 p.p.m. as a maximum and recommended later that this be dropped to 1 p.p.m. European hygienists are generally closer in their thinking to the Russian level than to American suggestions, and there is a good reason for this.

One would think that American viewpoints on chronic carbon monoxide effects, because of longer experience with overcrowded automotive traffic, would be better informed than European and Russian viewpoints. This is not the case. The reason is a a very curious one and one not readily admitted by American hygienists, who in fact almost invariably fail to call attention to it in their textbooks and learned papers. The reason is that during World War II chronic carbon monoxide poisoning became a sort of way of life, especially in the Scandinavian countries, because the automotive vehicles were run for a period of years on producer gas and charcoal gas instead of gasoline.

These fuels consist partly of CO to start with, hence it did not require any special malfunction of the engines to ensure that CO became an habitual component of the atmosphere of wartime Copenhagen, Stockholm, and Helsinki. Although reliable analytical data on atmospheric composition from these frantic days are not available, there is a wealth of clinical information from the studies by the Danish doctor, Grut, and the Finnish hygienist, Noro. There seems to be absolutely no doubt that chronic CO poisoning was suffered by thousands of Scandinavians, and indeed Noro recorded the incidence of 67.5 per cent of chronic cases among more than 5000 Finnish automobile and truck drivers whose vehicles operated on charcoal gas during the war years up through 1945.

In the standard American reference books (e.g., Dr. Frank Patty's *Industrial Hygiene and Toxicology*) there is no mention whatsoever of this European experience, which one might justifiably regard as the biggest source of information on chronic CO poisoning recorded throughout human history. (It is of interest, incidentally, that Patty is retired Director of the Department of Industrial Hygiene of General Motors Corporation.)

The viewpoint of American hygienists of the Patty school is that there is no such thing as chronic carbon monoxide poisoning.

The classical proof of this always turns out to be the "Holland tunnel experiment" carried out slightly before World War II, in which some traffic officers in New York City stationed at the exit of the Holland tunnel were examined and found to be in surprisingly adequate condition. There is a sort of heartiness and mysterious joviality with which American hygienists, especially those associated with the automotive industry, record that these splendid policemen, most of them thirteen years at the same spot, rich in carbon monoxide, suffered from nothing save perhaps occasional overweight, and were in better shape than any average group of men anywhere. Reading of the dauntless robustness of these massive guinea pigs, one begins to be sold on the idea that carbon monoxide should be pumped into offices to refresh the white-collar employees.

In discussing the differences between the American and Russo-European opinions on chronic CO poisoning, most of the American hygienists dismiss the conclusions arrived at by the Europeans and Russians as based on animal studies—white mice, dogs, rabbits—implying perhaps that the only proper experimental subjects are policemen. In view of the Scandinavian experience with chronic CO on a nationwide scale, where CO intoxication became for several years the most important occupational disease, this is of course utter nonsense. It is true, however, that the Russians and European standards have been influenced to a greater degree than have ours by studies of animals. The Russian change from a recommended maximum CO atmospheric content of 2 p.p.m. to 1 p.p.m., for instance, came from observations to the effect that mice exposed for long periods to 2 p.p.m. showed some barely perceptible evidence of brain damage.

The enormous chasm of disagreement between the two attitudes towards carbon monoxide: the American belief, for example, that not only is there no profit in talking about chronic CO poisoning, because New York traffic policemen don't suffer from it, but that concentrations of a hundred-fold higher than those the Russians regard as safe can be inhaled without any trouble, must somehow be bridged and a reconciliation of facts attained. We are talking of such high tonnages of CO that it is obvious that we must have worldwide agreement. More facts are needed before deciding on a set of standards, such as the one and a half per cent recent maximum CO regulation for modified automobile exhausts. If we do not need more facts, let us not *ignore* facts such as those in wartime Scandinavian studies.

It is purely rhetorical, of course, to imply that we do not need more facts. One of the reasons is that carbon monoxide by itself may act one way, while CO in the presence of other air pollutants may act better or worse. When it acts worse, this is called "synergism" or "potentiation." Carbon monoxide in the presence of nitric oxide (a common ingredient of auto exhaust gas) acts more viciously than it does by itself. It has been found that a submarine crew begins to suffer acute CO poisoning in the presence of one and a half percent carbon dioxide at a concentration level of CO that is much lower than would ordinarily cause the acute symptoms. This is probably because carbon dioxide at this level causes an increased respiration rate. This makes sense because in the case of resuscitation from CO poisoning a mixture of carbon dioxide with oxygen is more effective than oxygen alone. Hydrogen sulfide in amounts lower than fatal increases the rate at which CO can kill.

There is evidence that CO and gasoline or some components of gasoline are worse than CO alone, and the same thing has been observed with old-fashioned illuminating gas and attributed to the presence of small amounts of benzene as a synergist.

Doubtless there are other synergists but possibly there are also "anti-synergists"—compounds in the air which in small amounts may hinder the reaction between CO and hemoglobin. It would be important to establish this possibility, although it still might not explain the extraordinary unsinkability of the Holland tunnel policemen, since analysis of their blood showed fairly high amounts of carboxy-hemoglobin.

This brings up the important question of difference in sensitivity to CO poisoning. When exercising and thus breathing fast, the body is more quickly poisoned by a given amount of CO in the air, because the increased rate of respiration also causes chemical equilibrium to be reached faster, just as you get an equilibrium between an effervescent pill and a glass of water more quickly if you stir the water. Children, being normally more active than adults, are more rapidly overcome. But adults differ extraordinarily in their activity under rather standard conditions.

One person, waiting on the corner for a bus, will stamp about, spit, scratch, dart sudden looks around as if expecting any minute the arrival of a brilliant enemy. A self-conscious girl will develop special muscles interminably patting the back of her hair-do and utilizing that mysterious out-of-the-corner-of-the-eye alertness to males who are supposed to be staring at her hungrily. Other persons will stand as if asleep or in a state of hopelessness. The statistical swings of respiration and CO adsorption in the blood may thus be as wide as between the adults in the front seat of the car and the children playing on the floor in the back. These great variations of human behavior are overlooked in the statistics of hygienists, since hygienists are trained to exclude such *frivolia,* but they may explain the phenomena of the Holland tunnel experiment and other episodes.

Of course people with weak hearts, lung trouble, and invalids in general are more likely to be knocked out by CO than are cops, but this is true of any form of air pollution.

(That policemen are not invariably proof against chronic CO poisoning is shown by the recent case of a New Haven traffic cop, written up in *Time* magazine. This poor man chose unluckily to get away from his occupational hazard by spending a vacation walking behind a farm tractor.)

It should be mentioned that the party line of American hygienists is not shared by the whole U. S. medical profession, and among American believers in a chronic state of CO poisoning are some who have observed the following symptoms, most of which agree with the Scandinavian reports:

Headache, insomnia, fatigue, shortness of breath, nervousness, paresthesia (skin prickling), muscular twitching, emotionalism, nausea, drowsiness, unsteady gait, neuromuscular and joint pains, tremor, muscular cramps, cough, sweats, vomiting, loss of appetite, perversion of taste and smell, optic neuritis, loss of feeling in the forearms, decrease to sensitivity of pain in the little fingers, abnormal brain waves, speech defect, impairment of hearing, hoarseness and yawning.

It is axiomatic that any nervous person, looking over a list of symptoms for any disease, can immediately conclude: *Why that's exactly what I have!* From a statistical standpoint, however, it is interesting that this list includes most of the symptoms endured by heavy cigarette smokers.

This should not be surprising. It has been known for many years that smoking results in a very substantial inhalation of CO and formation of carboxy-hemoglobin in the blood. In fact, all modern studies of the effects of air pollution on human subjects have involved a distinction between smokers and non-smokers. Since the symptoms of chronic CO poisoning usually lag some hours behind the exposure to higher than normal CO concentrations, it is believed by some hygienists that hang-overs are to a large extent the result of excessive smoking rather than excessive consumption of alcohol. Adding to the persuasiveness of this theory is the fact that the hang-over victim is often benefited by breathing pure oxygen on the morning-after. As a service to bibulous travelers, many airports have made available doses of oxygen from slot machines.

Aside from the obvious external symptoms recorded, perhaps the most worrisome clinical finding is the Italian discovery of the reduction of Cytochrome C, especially in the heart.

(Cytochrome C is an iron-containing enzyme in the tissues that is rather similar to hemoglobin in chemical structure but which serves as a catalyst to help the tissues in their oxidation processes. From the standpoint of fundamental biochemistry, it is perhaps even more important than hemoglobin, since at higher pressures the whole body can get oxygen without hemoglobin, but it cannot use it without Cytochrome.)

Destruction of the cytochromes in crucial body tissues is the way cyanide kills.

Although the party-liners would like to look away from the fabulous tonnages of CO that accumulate in the air of Tokyo, New York, and other centers of combustion, it is evident that this nimbus is too huge for sensible people to ignore with jovial platitudes based on 30-year old medical surveys. If the party-liners are right and sub-lethal amounts of CO night and day have no more effect than simply living at a high altitude (say, Denver or Mexico City), then we could all literally breathe easier.

There are not enough accomplished facts to let us relax in this way. Here are some rather serious areas of ignorance represented by just enough preliminary information to under-line the questions:

What is the effect of temperature?

At 104°F—the average summer temperature of Needles, California—it has been found by Russian investigators that the toxic effect of CO is very severely increased. Furthermore (and this is really serious) the concentration of carboxy-hemoglobin in the blood no longer remains a measure of intoxication. Animals die at much lower doses of CO than they should. However, at the same temperature without CO their health is undamaged.

What is the effect of CO during pregnancy?

Recent French work shows that exposure of the mother to

abnormal CO concentrations during the seventh and ninth months can cause alteration of the child's brain structure.

Can people become "acclimatized" to higher than normal CO concentrations?

There is evidence that animals can. This may be the brightest hope in all the medical aspects of air pollution—the tough adaptive abilities of the human body.

Does the digestive system affect CO intoxication?

Italian research has shown that workers are much more susceptible to CO just after eating.

Can the body produce CO poisoning without breathing in CO?

Unfortunately for the clarification of the already complicated picture, this seems to be the case. In certain instances of diabetes and cardiovascular trouble, enough carboxy-hemoglobin can be found in the blood to be confused with chronic CO intoxication from without.

What is the relation between radiation sickness and CO?

Some very recent work indicates that mice exposed to high CO concentrations, right after very heavy x-ray treatment, showed much lower mortality to radiation disease. In this case CO appears to be a curative. This is all the more remarkable when it is realized that in radiation sickness CO is produced by the body and some of the symptoms are similar to those of CO poisoning. Unexpected findings of this sort prove how pitifully little we know about the body's chemistry and how desperately we are in need of more facts.

Does CO accumulate in the body only in combination with hemoglobin?

The party-liners would like everybody to believe so, but a very aggressive medical research group at the University of Naples finds that this is not true. After very prolonged exposure, the CO tends to be stored in some as yet unidentified way in the plasma of the blood. This is a very significant finding indeed and cuts the ground from under the exponents of the easy reversible theory of CO poisoning.

Do all the tissues of the body react in the same way to CO?

The simplified dogma of the party-liners would answer affirmatively, but new Russian and French studies indicate that the difference between oxygen content of arterial and venous blood (a critical number in CO intoxication) varies greatly. The difference shrinks to almost nothing in the brain but in most of the muscles the difference is, strangely, *increased*. This can only be explained by a secondary effect of CO in lowering the respiration of the brain but stimulating it in the muscles. Some living creatures might then be expected to react to CO poisoning like a chicken with its head cut off. Muscle twitching and automatic motions would survive black-out.

If we could cause the brain tissues to react as muscle tissues do, the rate of survival to acute attacks might be increased along with better resistance to chronic intoxication.

What does the spleen have to do with CO poisoning?

The spleen is an emergency organ. Although it is rather like a junkyard under ordinary conditions, where old and decrepit cells are taken apart and salvaged for their iron content, and the like, when the body is attacked by CO (or by anything else, for that matter) the spleen goes into a very rough over-time schedule. It produces red blood cells with hemoglobin—a job it normally does in human beings only in their embryo form.

The body's reaction to such an assault as CO poisoning is extremely complex, but one integrating battle-cry for all the other organs of the body is "Save the brain!" When good blood becomes scarce the whole vascular system contracts so that blood can be preserved for the brain. The spleen is normally simply packed with blood; as a reservoir, it contains a surprising fraction of all the blood in the body, but during the CO emergency, it unloads fast and makes more.

The nature and behavior of the spleen is, however, not thoroughly understood. For defense against the many air-pollution toxins which we will be discussing, it may turn out to be the key rallying point of the body.

chapter 5

THE ANATOMY OF RUIN

... eating the air on promise of supply ...

SHAKESPEARE, *King Henry IV*

In most of the air-pollution disasters mentioned we have emphasized that, although Man can accomplish wonders in poisoning the air he breathes (his masterpiece being the invention of cigarette smoking, which allows everyone to carry around with him his own personal air-pollution problem), he needs the help of geography and unnatural behavior of the air, if he is to put on a real horror show. If the air behaved itself, with continuous gentle breezes and if the warm air on the ground had colder air above, so that refreshing exchanges and ventilation could always take place, it would be as hard to poison a city as it would be to execute a man with hydrocyanic acid gas in a wind tunnel.

In order to understand our growing predicament, we need to know more about the habits of air—especially city air. The continuing Los Angeles crisis has stimulated a great study on air movements over large communities.

It has been found to be a misconception that you need a canyon or a bowl for a pollution build-up; a city on a plain has a characteristic surface roughness greater than its environs. The broad Kaw Valley in Kansas is faced with air pollution, although it is not so much a valley as a long low part in the plains which extends the entire length of the state and contains numerous cities. A city is a good *sink* for the energy of the air.

Just as Al Capp's little character carries along with him his own private thunder cloud, cities attract pools of relatively stagnant air. Within these pools, which can be fairly wide ones with internal eddy structures in the case of cities of very large area such as Houston, Oklahoma City, and Los Angeles, the movement of the air can be followed closely with devices which record even slight air motion and with tracers, the best of which is simply smoke. The use of such research tools has given rise to the concept of the "wind rose," which is a map of all the bulk air motions over a city at a given instant and at a given altitude. The wind roses at several altitudes give the full picture and along with the notion of the "trajectory" of a given parcel of air, tell the air-pollution expert just when angry telephone calls are going to start coming in from Pasadena after a truck of natural gas odorant blows up in Inglewood. Trajectories have been computed for the Los Angeles Basin from a 58-station network.

When there is no inversion, pollution is almost a poetic business. Consider the plumes of smoke from industrial sources or fires. They will rise to certain levels and drift downbreeze into long, laminated streamers. There will be hierarchies of such streamers. The plume from the bakery oven will stay demurely under the darker, more masculine plume from Joe Bloom's burning snack bar. The plumes will stay aloft during the night, whispering to each other, but will observe their vertical distances, and then about two hours after sunrise, all the streamers will be integrated downward and they will descend upon the city, perhaps thirty miles from their birthplaces. Since during the day the surface of the city heats up faster than the air level at which the portions of polluted air spent the night, the pollution will again be dissipated upward and, by the breezes, outward.

When there is a temperature inversion, all the stuff from countless sources of pollution will remain at ground level. In this sense, inversion simply increases the concentration of all the poisons which would always be produced but which would drift upward and outward. Nobody knows what causes a temperature inversion. The science of meteorology is one of the most complex and baffling ones, since it involves too many variables, even in pure places, uncontaminated by the doings of man. One thing that is certain is that cities do not *cause* temperature inversions. They do affect wind velocity, and unfavorably so for the horizontal dissipation of foul air, but inversions seem to be unpredictable, except to the extent that we do know that certain geographic localities will suffer them more often than others.

The history of temperature inversions, moreover, is clouded by the fact that until recently nobody paid any attention to them; and in fact it was not until the regular use of weather balloon and aircraft measurements that inversions could be directly demonstrated. Since that time, it has been shown that many cities that never heard of inversion-effected air pollution now must expect it, and have come to realize, in fact, that they had had it, but had not identified it.

Among large cities that have been hit by pollution troubles associated with inversion over the past few years are the following: Tokyo, Yokohama, Paris, London, Moscow, Leningrad, New York, Washington, Denver, San Francisco, Los Angeles, Buenos Aires, Vienna, Mexico City, Basel, Calcutta, Milan, Sydney, Osaka, etc., etc.

As a case history, I can recall that when I was a boy in Los Angeles, inversion must have been fairly common, although the place did not exude enough poisons to cause any complaint. Those clear days during which you could "see Catalina" (an island off the coast) were very scarce, and the picture of the Cahuenga Plain that you got from, say, Mount Wilson was generally of a placidly sprawled little city overhung with a rather becoming mistiness, like a light scarf on a woman's hair. Obviously the inversion was there, like a hidden psychosis, needing only about two million backyard trash burners and three million automobiles to bring about ruin.

Ruin can be avoided if a city is blessed often with rain. There is nothing that will clear up the foulness in the air as fast as rain. Portland, Oregon, is probably safe. This is also the reason why Dublin will never suffer, even if it becomes a megalopolis (as I hope it won't) and even if every Dubliner decides to burn a ton of King James Bibles every day in his backyard and spend the rest of the time scooting around in a smoking automobile.

From this point on we are going to make a clinical case of *"that city,"* El Pueblo de Nuestra Señora La Reina de Los Angeles de Porciúncula, not because it is my home town, but because there is more information about it, more fuss about it, and because it represents from the standpoint of smogsters the insidious pattern of what all cities now fear they can become.

Smog in Los Angeles first became a public issue during World War II and was immediately blamed on a government-financed attempt to make butadiene for synthetic rubber on the part of the Southern California Gas Company, which had put into action a sort of bailing-wire-constructed plant down in the industrial section. The plant never amounted to anything, but there is no doubt that it did make a lot of smells for a short time. When it was closed down, and the smog symptoms continued even worse, the Rubber Reserve breathed a sigh of relief, but the smog detectives were disappointed. Suspicion shifted suddenly to the oil companies.

THE BREATH OF LIFE

I can recall at this time walking back from lunch at the University Club with two oil company executives to the office in the midst of real smog. One could see the office building vaguely two blocks ahead in a sort of hot blue halo, and I timidly suggested, between coughs, that this was awful. They were both men of formidable stature and they looked down at me through eyes streaming with tears. "What? What's awful?" they gasped. "What are you talking about?"

What *was* I talking about? This was no London fog, and it didn't smell like sulfuric acid, but it made the eyes sting like the effluvia from hot, dry, freshly-cut onions. Years later, when I was in another place, I sent a young chemist out to Los Angeles on an assignment having nothing to do with smog. He was from Arkansas and had never been in Los Angeles. He stayed the night at a downtown hotel which was sufficiently luxurious to afford what they call "internal overpressure"; in other words, the inside of the hotel was protected against air pollution by keeping the air pressure slightly above that of the streets outside. Blithely and with typical energy on a smoggy morning the young man pushed through the sealed doors out into the atmosphere; the smog hit him and instantly blinded him and he fell over a baby carriage. I am happy to report that the baby was unharmed (at least by my friend), but the chemist skinned his shin badly.

We will have a good deal to say later in regard to why people cry in such smogs, but in the meantime something should be said of visibility. Stanford Research Institute, after a good many years of investigation, concluded that the visibility in California smogs is a question of the concentration of "particulate matter" in the air; that is, it is smoke, or haze, but it is not London-type smoke. Extremely small particles constitute the visibility block. They are so small, in fact, that it would be next to impossible to filter them out of the air, even if billions of dollars were available for such an attempt. In downtown Los Angeles, 90 per cent of these particles are said to come from man-made pollution and 10 per cent from "natural haze." (Since nobody is yet prepared to state exactly what "natural haze" consists of in a large city, one can draw the conclusion that this was the lady's scarf I used to see as a small boy from Mt. Wilson, and simply consisted of smog below the level of insistent squawks.)

Visibility had been getting poor even in the early 1930's ("the smog-free years") with a population only one-half that in 1950. In summer and early fall it was very seldom that visibility in these depression years exceeded twelve miles.

But it was the acrid smell and the eye-hurting that set off the uproar.

About the time that the City Fathers and the rich old ladies of Pasadena were prepared to blame it all on the neighboring petroleum refineries, there emerged one of the most fantastic smog theories of all time—one that blamed everything on a freak of nature that would probably go away if we all prayed hard enough. This was the theory that smog originated somewhere off the coast, out there beyond Santa Catalina Island, because out there the ozone along the nitrogen oxides from high altitudes descended to the ocean suddenly on dark nights and at capricious intervals and blew in over the Los Angeles Basin during the day. The author of this theory claimed that since early times, even in the eighteenth century, "brownish fumes" had been observed around San Pedro and Long Beach sneaking in from the sea.

It is incredible to note the popularity of this childish notion, which has taken many years of time on the part of serious men to demolish, even though it could so easily have been demolished through the observations of any native that San Pedro,

Long Beach, and the other coastal communities didn't have any smog. The scientifically uninitiated, for whom the concept of the ozonosphere and of high-altitude nitrogen oxides was a little too complicated, still seized upon the idea of the mess originating from "out there beyond Catalina," perhaps instigated by Japanese, or even by San Franciscans.

In time, however, the oil refineries became the standard scapegoats, and during the early postwar period there were serious proposals actually to shut down the refineries. This was a time of exasperation and unreason. The oil companies made major and commendable efforts to take the curse off by eliminating all trace of sulfurous fumes and smoke from their operations, but nothing seemed to satisfy the people of Pasadena.

For anybody who has been through the wringer, those sessions of trying to talk sensible facts to smog-enraged councilmen and retired people from Toledo and Peoria seems now to have been a nightmare of futility.

But almost overnight, it seems, the monkey was suddenly on the back of the automobile. (This switch was not too drastic for the anti-petroleum people, since they could still blame the oil companies for producing fuel that the automobile couldn't digest.) The automobile had been a villain "on deck," so to speak, all along, since as early as World War I days, when the belief was expressed that automobiles were too smelly and noisy for a paradise such as Southern California. Furthermore, the early days of diesel-engine buses in the city focused attention on the particularly skunky odor of their exhaust smoke. In fact, in the early 1930's the municipal bus company bought diesel fuel from the oil companies on the basis of a curious competitive procedure: the different test fuels delivered in coded cans were tested in separate buses that were driven around a corner on which stood a panel of sniffing persons, who marked the exhaust quality. The fuel which gave the least acrid exhaust got its supplier the contract for the coming year. This is probably not the least of the reasons for a still stubborn belief that some magical refining process will also take the curse out of gasoline engine exhausts.

More than odor was involved. When a lady with nylon hose happened to be engulfed in diesel-bus exhaust, she frequently suffered the embarrassment of having her stockings fall away in shreds. In fact, it was damage to materials rather than to human noses and lungs that concentrated the spotlight on exhaust chemicals in general. When rubber tires were stacked in warehouses in Los Angeles the tires on the bottom usually were found to have developed cracks, and indeed it is Professor Haagen-Smit's "stress cracking" of rubber test which is still the most reliable method of estimating the ozone content of city air.

Realistic merchants have been aware, especially in England, of the out-of-pocket costs of air pollution. As the result of the 1952 London smog, a chain store had to reduce in one day the prices of its damaged goods by 90,000 pounds, and the Beaver Report in 1954 estimated the total annual economic loss because of English smog at 250 million pounds. In this country estimates as early as 1949 were that the annual loss because of materials damaged by air pollution was $1.5 billion or about $10 per person. (The estimate would now be much higher.)

A curious sidelight on smog damage is that paper made before 1750 is not seriously damaged by smogs containing sulfur dioxide, but paper made by modern chemical processes and exposed to smog loses folding resistance and becomes very brittle. This is because metals in the chemically processed paper catalyze the conversion of the sulfur dioxide to sulfuric acid. As we will see later, this loss in "folding resistance" is not unlike the same effect of air pollution on the human lungs, when emphysema is the end result.

There are also some less tangible but none the less discouraging effects of air pollution on statuary, classical ruins, frescoes, and ancient buildings. This would not be important in Los Angeles, where to my knowledge the only statue of note was a rather bloated cherub located in Pershing Square. However, in cities of greater public reverence for the arts of sculpture and architecture air pollution has become a destroyer of beloved relics. Recently it has caused great concern in New York City, London, Florence, Paris, Athens—nearly all the cities containing outdoor objects or buildings of historical or aesthetic value and where sulfur dioxide or aerosol smogs of the familiar London type are becoming more common. In great cities where the air is dry and warm, such as Cairo and New Delhi, air pollution in this context is not so much of a problem.

There is a curious thing about classical statuary. Having created such achingly beautiful sculptural objects and in very large numbers in the pre-Christian days, man himself deliberately destroyed a large part of them and now is indirectly destroying a good part of the rest of them (at least that part which remains out-of-doors due to size or other reasons) with sulfurous fumes. It is seldom realized that during the early medieval period, the Greek and Roman statues or ruins were not looked upon with admiration but were regarded simply as heathen offal. However, the medieval masons knew pure limestone when they saw it, and they needed it to make plaster finishes. Marble is the purest form of limestone and hence lime-burners of the Middle Ages had no hesitation in burning in their kilns what would now amount to billions of dollars' worth of classical marble statues to make plaster having better adhesive properties for houses and beer halls. (One must admit that later in this era some of the priceless lime went into parts of equally beautiful Gothic cathedrals.) Before this, vandals had taken the jeweled eyes from Greek statues, and the polychromatic paints which Phidias had used on his Chryselephantine sculptures had succumbed early in the sad story of man's long lapse into semi-savagery. The colors were applied in combination with terra-cotta finishes —blue, yellow, different shades of red, mauve, touches of gilding; mostly the colors flaked off, leaving only the drab buff of the terracotta, but where they have survived in spots one gets a tantalizing peek at the gay, harmonious magic that the Greeks were able to evoke from their quarried rock. Now we find twentieth-century man completing the ruin of out-of-doors classical art, even of Renaissance and Medieval Christian art, with fumes from the burning of high-sulfur middle-eastern fuel oil and from the exhausts of automobile engines.

Sulfur dioxide and the aerosols are chemically corrosive for all types of limestone. The stone powders, crumbles, flakes, cracks, or chips. In Rome the Colosseum, the Arch of Titus and many frescoes are in danger. Even without the sulfurous fumes of modern industry, weathering (especially frost) causes stone to decay by freezing of water in the outside pores of the stone, making it crack. Vitruvius, the greatest of the ancient Roman architects, was aware of the fact that there are different grades of limestone of varying resistance to aging, and in his remarkable manual of building-construction written during the reign of Augustus (27 B.C.–A.D. 14), he has some shrewd suggestions:

"Let the stone be got out two years before, in summer but not in winter, and let it lie in exposed places. Those stones, which in this time are damaged by weathering, are to be thrown into the foundations. Those which are not faulty are tested by Nature, and can endure when used in building above ground."

These differences in chemical resistance are well known

today. Some of the Strasbourg Cathedral, for example, is deteriorating rapidly, yet other sections are in relatively good condition. The Washington Monument, which has undergone its first cleaning in thirty years, turns out to be lighter colored in the lower third of the shaft, since different strata of marble from the same quarry were used for its construction.

A striking contrast between the surface health of ancient buildings in Britain affected by differing qualities of air can be seen by visiting Oxford and Cambridge Universities. The city of Oxford has become industrialized and its automobile traffic very heavy. After a pleasant night of dining and wining at the venerable Mitre Hotel, one is awakened at dawn by the sort of ear-rending High Street noises one hears at 42nd and Broadway. Accordingly, in this "sweet city of dreaming spires," the storied towers and ivied walls of the charming old Colleges of the University, built mostly of limestone from the Cotswolds, have taken on the typical patina and erosion of sulfurous smudge; one's first instinct is to grab a mop and pail and have at them. On the other hand, the Cambridge structures, of the same type of limestone, remain pristine and clean. The reasons are obvious: although Cambridge is approaching Oxford in both industry and motor traffic, the University still is sufficiently remote from both to permit its façades some expectation of life in the future.

The ancient Greek sometimes used resins as protective coatings. Today the principal waterproofing technique is to spray or brush on silicic acid or synthetic resins. Another is to impregnate the stone with beeswax. It is doubtful that these measures are well advised, since they may do more harm than good. A silica or wax coating prevents the stone from breathing and moisture can get trapped beneath the surface layer and in winter, by freezing, can cause the surface to crack.

It is obvious that the only safe thing to do with precious

stone objects in these days of corrosive air is to place them indoors. André Malraux in France has been the most aggressive preserver of "les vieilles pierres," the externally located statues being removed to shelter and replaced by plaster casts. But one cannot do this with massive buildings. In Florence the Ponte Vecchio, the Pitti Palace, the Palazzo Strozzi and the Basilica of San Lorenzo are suffering disastrous deterioration. Washing the sulfuric acid off with water is a possible safeguarding measure but is terribly expensive for large structures. It costs $100,-000 to water-wash a cathedral.

Careful repair of damaged stone is an art or a profession, something like dentistry. Thus the Acropolis is checked minutely with brushes every day, since the modern Greeks fully realize the equity in tourist money embodied in this breath-taking ruin. In West Germany the Ruhr state of Westphalia is spending four million dollars a year on special preservation methods for cathedrals and other historic structures. Westphalia is alert also to the automotive exhaust menace. On days when the smog is critical, the use of private cars is outlawed for four hours in both mornings and afternoons.

The worldwide air pollution has justifiably spawned some worried official groups, such as the Conservation Center of New York University's Institute of Fine Art. The International Council of Museums, a branch of UNESCO, is making a worldwide survey of stone decay. What is needed is an expert subgroup of protesters, to insist on the removal of sources of sulfurous smog. Here lower sulfur specifications on fuel oils would be helpful, although judging by the horrified screams of industrial fuel-users provoked in New York City by such a suggestion, the way will not be an easy one.

As an appendix to the story of the effect of air pollution on statuary and other outdoor precious material, we should direct some attention to pigeons. In "pigeon-cities" (and San Francisco, New York, and Venice come to mind) it is regarded as only slightly less bestial to carry out any form of pigeon liquidation than to strangle human infants. This hardy and extroverted bird has an extremely short lower bowel and his digestive processes, although smooth and efficient, result in frequent defecations. He prefers to defecate on churches and statues of saints and heroes. Since he is monstrously overfed in the cities that dispense to him bread crumbs and stale cake and cookies, the periods between his interminable meals and his bowel movements become as short as his flight from the ground level of a park or a street to a beloved religious monument.

The chief component of the pigeon's dropping is uric acid, which can corrode stone as well as make it look like a very spotty whitewash job. Furthermore there is evidence that pigeon droppings, when finely dispersed in the air by wind, can provoke human ailments, such as brain damage by a fungus in the bird excrement known as *cryptococcus neoformans*. Mites that thrive on the droppings cause human skin eruptions, and the U.S. Public Health Service has warned against histoplasmosis from pigeon excreta. In its milder forms, this causes cold symptoms and in its acute stage, death.

The problem of weeding out the pigeon population seems insurmountable. There are very few pressure groups as fierce and adamant as those of the bird lovers. The Bird Guardian's League in San Francisco, for example, would like to increase the pigeon population to the ratio of New York City, which is approximately five million pigeons to eight million human beings. Any proposals to weed out these air-pollution vectors is met not with wailing but with ferocious threats. They emphasize that they have a lot of votes and, in many cases, a lot of money.

It is a strange society that allows a robust, parasitic, and unlovely bird to outweigh the good of humankind.

Protesting for other reasons has been developed in the great smog cities into a diverting sideshow of mass psychology, and the progression of protesting in Los Angeles provides an especially interesting clinical history.

The gradual nomination of the automotive engine as the chief offender in Los Angeles' smog was received with very little enthusiasm either on the part of Detroit or of the gasoline producers. A reasonable counterattack on their part was to blame smog instead on the peculiar backyard trash-burning habits of the city. It was true enough that the smogs had grown in intensity and frequency with the enormous increase in the car population, but the amount of trash burned in poorly controlled private incinerators had also increased astronomically.

Simply burning the throw-away local newspapers and supermarket bulletins could be expected to engulf a smaller city in smoke. Serious treatises have been written on modern trash and especially on paper trash, which now represents an absurdly high proportion of the energy content of civilization. One has only to think of the percentage of lower class mail the average citizen receives which winds up immediately in the waste basket on its way to incineration and dispersal in the atmosphere, to realize that this represents a peculiar national dilemma. So huge a quantity of printed paper, mostly conveying no essential or even meaningful information, is probably the best example of what scientists call "entropy"—the degradation of higher to lower forms of energy and of more to less complex chemical structure, in this case to fire and tarry particles in the communal air. Publishers of books and even newspapers make very little money, but printing companies make a great deal and paper companies never had it so good.

This sort of paper comprised the heaviest load on the Los

Angeles backyard incinerator, but of course the load was spiced with twigs, hedge cuttings, discarded girdles, sorry old socks, combustible plastic junk, and not infrequently with dead kittens —all the offal that the respectable incombustible trash collector refused to accept, which meant his average take-away consisted mostly of tomato and beer cans and empty Vodka bottles.

In due time city and county ordinances put a stop to this. Combustible trash was collected and burned in great glossily engineered systems of furnaces which allowed not one speck of smoke or odor to escape to the hungry air.

The Los Angeles smogs continued worse than ever.

The fact was now accepted that this was because there were more automobiles than ever. From a rather forlorn post mortem statistical analysis, it was shown that the incidence of serious smogs had simply followed with mathematical exactitude the increase of the car population, ever since smog had become a dirty name in Southern California. This is not quite correctly stated, and the degree of incorrectness makes an even more overwhelming case against the automobile, because it could be demonstrated that it was not the number of cars but the amount of driving; during those special few war years of gasoline rationing in Los Angeles, the smogs were less frequent.

To a chemist, it now seems incredible that this should not have been realized earlier. The internal combustion engine is a small chemical factory. Theoretically what it is supposed to do is to oxidize hydrocarbons to carbon dioxide and water, both of them wholesome, familiar compounds. However, this is not what the engine does in practice. A lot of extremely complicated chemical reactions take place in the process of exploding a mixture of gasoline and air. It is true that under normal engine conditions these reactions result in only barely detectable amounts of queer stuff in the exhaust. But unfortunately the air pollution mess that we are in is a matter of barely detectable amounts of queer stuff. Smog chemists live in a world of "parts per million" or even "parts per billion."

Furthermore, under abnormal conditions (which can simply mean a second-hand car with bad sparkplugs or a faulty carburetor), the engine can pour out almost anything. At the 1963 World Petroleum Congress, a Japanese chemical engineering team showed how a six-cylinder piston engine could be run on natural gas to make a mixture of nearly pure carbon monoxide and hydrogen, which can later be catalytically converted to ammonia or methyl alcohol. The Japanese had figures to show that this was a cheaper way to make so-called "synthesis gas" than the usual high-pressure reactors, because you get some by-product power from the reaction that can be converted to electricity.

This concept of the automobile engine as a versatile chemical plant has revolutionized our way of thinking of modern smog problems, and in fact our way of thinking of combustion in general. In the following chapters we shall examine this depressing versatility of the automotive engine, especially in its clinical aspects.

chapter 6

TEAR GAS AND
SPINACH KILLERS

Not green the foliage but of dusky hue . . .
No fruits therein, but thorns with poison grew.

DANTE, *Divine Comedy*

In late August and early September of 1955 in Los Angeles
the temperature averaged over 100°F for more than a week and
severe smog occurred. The death rate rose alarmingly. People
who were hot and whose eyes hurt suddenly began to panic.
The Question which buzzed around was: "Can this smog *kill*
us?" There was a chorus of soothing editorials in the local newspapers, and consolation came in the historical recollection that
during a similar hot spell in 1939, when it was over 100°F
right down on the Long Beach seashore, the mortality had been
even higher and there had been no smog. Just good, simple
heat was killing the old, the frail, and the native Californians
who were unaccustomed to and unprepared for the brutal Mid-
dlewestern type of heat.

It is true that Southern California has always been unprepared
for anything—hot spells, earthquakes, brush fires, floods, gangster invasions, blonde hopheads, or wartime air raids. The
nature of the place is that it is in a chronic state of unreadiness.
Perhaps this is part of its helpless female charm. Defense against
natural disasters has always taken the form of *ex post facto* de-
nials, in the newspapers and by the Junior Chamber of Com-

merce, that any such disasters ever took place. News statisticians now know, for example, that only a fraction of the fatalities in the Long Beach earthquake of 1933 or the great flood of 1934 were ever owned up to by the local journals. This has introduced a curious dualism in public information. Scientists and statisticians have one set of figures; the local public has another.

However, the public still knows when its eyes hurt. Since the graver implications of air pollution have always been ignored in favor of spectacular annoyances, a great deal more research has gone into the problems of eye irritation and vegetable damage than of such matters as chronic lung disease and heart trouble. This is the reason for the procession to dignity of the "olefin theory" of Los Angeles smog.

Olefins are certain hydrocarbons resulting from automobile exhausts and, to put it simply, they are compounds that are missing some hydrogen in their molecules to the extent that they are hungry to react with something. There are a lot of things around with which they can react. The Los Angeles air in effect says to the olefin "Be my guest! Don't be a lonely heart!" and provides the olefin molecule with congenial company such as nitrogen oxides, ozone, chemical fragments known as free radicals, even ions. The olefins can react with nitrogen oxides through a rather complicated series of sunlight-induced mechanisms which wind up in forming what was long known as "Compound X." It is now identified as "peroxyacetylnitrate," and there is no doubt that it will make people cry, but it is by no means the only lachrymatory agent in the smog. Common smog ingredients that are known as aldehydes, particularly formaldehyde and acrolein, also brings tears, and we cannot lose sight of our old London friend, the sulfuric aerosols, which are also powerful eye irritants, but are probably minor nuisances in the air of a city that burns no coal. There is, however, the possibility that the aerosols weaken the eye's resistance to the aldehydes and the other more subtle arrows of the air.

The depressing thing to smog scientists is that elaborate tests with all the materials mentioned still do not identify any one of them or a known combination of them as the actual chemical criminal in eye distress. Synthetic smog, produced by mixing chemicals in a test chamber, is not real smog, and countless tests with undergraduates as guinea pigs have left Stanford University scientists only with a feeling of distrust for Stanford undergraduates or sometimes with a feeling that there are some things in the world that are simply too complicated to deal with.

The clinical side of the picture, however, is not frightening. There appears to be no permanent damage to eyes. Studies by various medical teams have shown that, although eye irritation affects about three-quarters of the population in the metropolitan areas of Southern California, no serious chronic trouble has been reported or can be expected. One peculiar and unexpected finding is that ozone (which is otherwise so dangerous that we will devote a whole chapter to it) has no disturbing effect on the eye. In fact, the development of a large excess of ozone during a Los Angeles "alert" always signals a rapid decline in eye irritation. The irritant, whatever it is, has been nearly exhausted, and the growing ozone concentration proceeds to knock it out completely. Thus the crying phase of smog has by that time passed into a really toxic phase.

Although some of the chemicals which result in weeping can be ignored as causes of anything save annoyance to natives and good business for ophthalmologists, the effects of the same chemicals on plant life cannot so easily be shrugged off. Plants are the innocent bystanders in man-made air pollution, and like innocent bystanders everywhere they have a knack for being hurt.

One by no means need confine the tragedy of plant damage to California. Perhaps the most dramatic example of what air pollution (in this case sulfur dioxide) can do to a countryside is the so-called "little desert" of Ducktown, Tennessee, near a group of smelters. Vegetation has refused to grow thereabouts for over half a century.

Perhaps because sulfur dioxide is one of the oldest of air pollutants (being produced in volcanic emissions), modern plants have developed a valiant defense mechanism against it. Most plants can tolerate exposure to sulfur dioxide below a threshhold concentration indefinitely, since the cells in the leaf stomata have the capacity to detoxify it by conversion to sulfate. However, the process of plant evolution never anticipated the amounts of sulfur dioxide that man would pour into the air. When the threshhold is exceeded, as it is around smelters and the like, sulfite builds up inside the plant's leaves, the water relations of the cells are disrupted and the plant collapses with the dramatic suddenness of a man keeling over from coronary thrombosis.

Other air pollutants will kill plants with much less trouble. Hydrofluoric acid, for example, as a not uncommon poison near some ore-dressing and petroleum-refining operations, will kill certain plants at one-thousandth of the concentration at which sulfur dioxide will do the job. Ozone will kill plants at extraordinarily low concentrations, and this includes tobacco plants, in New Jersey and Connecticut. A serious attempt has been made to breed ozone-resistant strains of tobacco.

Ethylene, a relatively harmless ingredient of city smogs as far as humans are concerned, is very tough on many plants, especially orchids; this has been a recent affliction around San Francisco, where orchid growers had retired in disgust from Southern California. It has been for some years impossible, on account of smog, to grow either orchids or spinach in the Los Angeles area.

Plant injury has become a matter of extensive litigation. The so-called "hidden injury" claim has become a lawyer's bonanza. A shaky distinction has been drawn between "injury," implying all the physiological upsets arising from air pollution, and "damage," referring to those effects which make a plant inedible or useless in a commercial sense.

Citrus tree "quick decline" in the smoggy parts of Southern California has been justifiably blamed on air pollution. The trees lose their leaves too early, grow poorly and yield small fruit. Full-grown trees age prematurely. Crabapple trees in New Jersey show the same sickliness, and air pollution in that state is blamed for poor yields of alfalfa and a decline in violets. (It is so long since a violet was ever seen to survive in Los Angeles that the natives hardly recognize the flower.)

Recently it has been found that plants can absorb without harm some chemicals that are very unwholesome for man. This is true of lead, which is found to be a normal constituent of plants growing along highways, where they are exposed to the tetraethyl lead residues from the exhaust of automobiles. Canadian public health authorities are checking what they consider a possible correlation between contamination of roadside plant crops with several diseases.

As in the case of eye irritations, not all the polluting chemicals responsible for damage to plants have been identified. There is a feeling, becoming general among biologists, that the sum is greater than its parts. This is because of the phenomenon known as "synergism," in which two or more chemicals acting together can produce a much greater effect than could be predicted from the results of any one chemical by itself. We will have much more to say about this, since it involves the very heart of the question of air-pollution hazard to man. The most unsettling aspect of synergism is that a combination of pollutants may not only have more effect than the pollutants alone but may have a different effect. Thus while chemicals A and B separately might cause, let us say, sneezing, A and B together might cause a heart attack. Fortunately there are not uncommon cases of "negative synergism": one chemical counteracts the effect of the other. This was true, as mentioned earlier, where the baby's wet ammoniacal diapers protected him against sulfuric aerosols, and the incompetence of stable janitors saved the lives of prize cattle in London.

Another crucial problem in the effect of air pollutants on plants as well as animals, including man, is that of the *cumulative* nature of the exposure. It appears that the orchids and spinach of Los Angeles did not all die in the first bad smog. However, periodic exposure to two decades of smog had such a high incidence of mortality that people just stopped trying to raise orchids and spinach. The resistance of different species of plants to smog varies strangely, and this variation extends to resistance to temporary high concentrations of a vicious killer such as ozone as well as resistance over a period of time to the less deadly materials such as ethylene.

Horticulturists and home gardeners in California have become diagnosticians. The dry sepal damage to orchids caused by ethylene is unmistakable to a San Franciscan, and this sympton should be carefully noted by Rex Stout's Nero Wolfe, since New York is becoming a smog area. In most sensitive plants Los Angeles smog causes a cross-leaf banding rather than the blotching or streaking that the London horticulturist will observe because of sulfur dioxide.

I was brought up in a canyon in the northern environs of Los Angeles, where it was popular to grow Ragged Robin roses. This delightful plant has vanished from the canyon now. Its contribution to the canyon's once typical bouquet of eucalyptus trees, honeysuckle, and sage, has been taken over by the smell of scorched rubber as the boys whiz up and down Glen Albyn Drive and as the temperature inversions press the exhaust effluvia of hundreds of thousands of whizzing boys' fourth-hand jalopies into the canyon's throat, as one would put a chloroform-soaked towel to the face of a lovely old lady.

So much for nostalgia, since our objective is to examine smog in all its clinical generalities and to find out what can be done about it; but I call attention to this ruined canyon of my youth, since hundreds of both sober and gay cities throughout the world, which now believe themselves free to raise Ragged Robin roses and violets and orchids and even spinach, if that is their pleasure, will find such pleasures denied them before the end of the century.

As you watch a skid-row alcoholic supine on the sidewalk with some degree of concern that the bell could also someday toll for you, if you don't take care, you should watch poor Los Angeles with some shared solicitude for all cities, including maybe your own, whose air-flow patterns will make them eventual victims of the automobile. Twenty-five per cent of all the air-pollution technicians and officials of the United States are now located in Los Angeles. The city is making a brave attempt to get to its feet, but the present attempt is not going to be enough. What is needed is not smelling salts but a series of desperate surgical operations, the nature of which we will consider in later chapters.

chapter 7

THE VILLAIN WITH THE
SHARP KNIFE

. . . a strangling air. . . .

C. DAY LEWIS, *Newsreel*

Years and years ago (before everything got sticky and dangerous—like maybe before World War I) ozone was regarded as a
synonym for fresh air; more than that, in a sort of poetic
return to the centuries of alchemy, as a symbol of the very
breath of life. In Wilmington, California, there is an Ozone
Avenue and probably there are hundreds of Ozone Avenues
and even boulevards named after this supposedly benign god-
dess of the atmosphere. A man in 1910 who felt the need
would say, "I'm going out and get a little ozone." He would
mean that he wanted to refresh himself with the air of early
morning. Today, especially in the smog-haunted cities, his
friends might well assume that his intention was to commit
suicide. It would be a dirty and agonizing kind of death.

What is ozone? Its chemical formula is deceptively simple: O_3.
This means that three oxygen atoms are congregated where only
two should be. If one saw ozone as an atmosphere in itself,
it would be light blue in color. Somebody has described its
unforgettable odor as the way the fillings in your teeth taste
when you are being electrocuted.

Ozone has so much energy packed in its strained molecule
that it has been an object of frustrated longing on the part of

rocket-propellant chemists, who can figure out on paper that a mixture of concentrated ozone with practically anything (even an old human lung) would give such a lively thrust to a booster rocket that we would have the Russians beaten. The highest temperature we know how to make with chemicals alone is the burning of cyanogen or cyanogenlike fuels with pure ozone—temperatures higher than the surface of the sun. Unfortunately, concentrated ozone, even without cyanogen or an old lung or any other companion to react with, wants so desperately to explode that it will explode with itself under the slightest excuse. It will react slowly with various compounds to form "ozonides," which are still so explosive that in places where ozone is being made and purified, even in the front office one is not allowed to use a fly-swatter and is discouraged from thoughtfully tapping a pencil on a desk.

It has been mentioned that ozone in its proper place (80,000 feet up in the air) is our guardian angel, since its formation and destruction by ultraviolet light not only protects us against the sun, which would like to wipe us out, but the dissociation reaction liberates heat so that the warm belt at these altitudes helps maintain the thermal equilibrium of the planet. At ground levels in the air we breathe, ozone is a blue devil.

Ozone in smog was first played up by a great chemist, Professor Haagen-Smit of Cal Tech, a Dutchman who started out as a plant physiologist and who wound up as "Dr. Smog." No man in history has contributed more to the knowledge of the chemistry of modern automobile air pollution, which to a large extent is the chemistry of ozone at ground level.

In the reactions that result in the formation of ozone under smog conditions, we are at the heart of our dilemma. The readers must bear with me, if they can, since the chemistry is so subtle and so unfamiliar that it represents possibly the most perplexing and complex technical problem that men have ever faced. The possible exception is the chemistry of life itself—and that may also be involved.

We shall start with some assumptions about the way internal combustion engines operate, although a closer and more bilious look will be devoted to this subject in the next-to-the-last chapter when we shall suggest that the use of these engines be restricted.

What seems to happen is this:

ACT I:

A small part of the nitrogen in the air that mixes with the motor fuel in the carburetor reacts with oxygen at the high-pressure and high-temperature part of the engine cycle. This forms nitric oxide (NO). At the same time, due to imperfections of operation that are inherent to any combustion system as complex as an automotive engine, a small part of the fuel avoids being completely burned and, either in unchanged or partly oxidized form, is exhausted along with the nitric oxide.

ACT II:

The sunlight now is able to work on a fine mess of chemicals, but in this mess we must realize that the nitric oxide is the key criminal. We must not let it get away into the crowd. The nitric oxide will react rather promptly with air or oxidizing constituents of the air (even without light), to form some nitrogen dioxide (NO_2). Now the fun begins.

ACT III:

Under the influence of ultraviolet light a fast so-called "equilibrium reaction" sets in between oxygen and nitrogen dioxide to give ozone and nitric oxide. An equilibrium reaction is one that occurs in both directions simultaneously, so that while ozone and nitric oxide are being produced in one direction, nitrogen dioxide and oxygen are being re-formed in the other direction. Chemists write it this way:

$$NO_2 + O_2 \rightleftarrows O_3 + NO$$
(ultraviolet light)

This process is one of the most crucial on the face of the earth, and if you never see or hope to see another chemical equation, you still may want to remember this one.

It would be simple if this seemingly clear-cut equilibrium were the whole ozone story. It is not; in fact, the situation is so complicated it is positively flabbergasting.

In the first place, the air contains the fuel residues and partly oxidized fuel that ozone likes to react with. The astonishing thing is that the presence of these substances does not *decrease* the amount of ozone but *increases* it. Ozone goes on building up to concentrations that it would never attain if one had no organic matter in the air.

A mishmash of photochemical side reactions takes place in which, for example, nitric oxide reacts with partly oxidized fuel to form "Compound X" (the tear-causing peroxyacetyl-nitrate), which in turn photochemically decomposes to give nitrogen dioxide. Thus a feedback mechanism is provided to give more NO_2 and continue producing more ozone. This isn't the half of it, and even this half is more speculation than proven fact. Scores of things are happening at the same time.

However, there is this to remember. Smog of this type is a disease of the daytime. At night the whole cycle subsides. Furthermore, certain fuel products from the car exhausts undoubtedly promote the formation of more excess ozone in a given period of time than others. Certain olefins (hydrocarbons lacking a full quota of hydrogen in their structure) will bring the ozone concentration to a peak in less than one hour of sunlight. This was the reason for the olefin furor in Los Angeles that resulted in stipulating by law a maximum in the olefin content of gasolines, on the theory that part of the fuel which went through the engine completely unburned would at least be relatively harmless. This has some element of rationality but unfortunately the engine has a habit of producing olefins from non-olefins, and indeed in some cases it picks on the most harmless-seeming fully saturated fuel to convert to olefins. Furthermore, the saturated hydrocarbons themselves result in ozone buildup, but simply over a longer period of time (perhaps eight to ten hours instead of less than one). Thus even if all the olefins could miraculously be removed from all the exhaust pipes, on a bright summer day in Los Angeles, there would still be ozone in the afternoon. Still more discouraging is the evidence that this ozone peak might be higher than the quick peaks caused by olefins.

We thus seem to be stuck with ozone unless something much more drastic than changing gasoline specifications is done. The question is, what does ozone do to us?

Very few direct medical experiments with human beings have been carried out, and for a good reason: it is like experimenting with a poison gas. The experiments with animals have not been reassuring.

Up to about 1957, it was the erroneous opinion that just a short spell of ozone wouldn't hurt anybody and might even be beneficial. As a result of the brilliant and methodical investigations of such smog biologists as Stokinger, it is now known that a level of six parts per million in air ozone will kill practically any laboratory animal within four hours. Death is caused by lung edema and hemorrhage. Young animals are the most susceptible; day-old chicks die almost instantly. Intermittent exposure is less dangerous than steady exposure. The acuteness of ozone attacks is increased greatly by (a) exercise, (b) alcohol in the system and (c) increased temperature. During the summer a concentration of only two parts per million is fatal to rats. On the the other hand, the severity of ozone is decreased by (a) previous exposure (thus first-time visitors to Los Angeles are much more susceptible than the old-timers), (b) previous injections of ascorbic acid (Vitamin C), (c) previous exposure of the lungs to oil mists; for example, a mist of cycloparaffinic mineral oil (Nujol).

Cumulative effects of exposure to less than lethal amounts of ozone may be very serious in that they can bring to a head latent respiratory infections. Animals with slight lung congestions can be killed easily by ozone. One would guess that an easy way to succumb to ozone would consist of being a child alcoholic, arriving with a snootful and a slight case of virus pneumonia for the first time in Los Angeles on a hot, smoggy day and running all the way from the airport to the Beverly-Hilton Hotel.

The sharp-knife effect of ozone is all the more remarkable when you consider that once ozone has been inhaled, it is so reactive that only about one-quarter of it gets by the nasal and bronchial passages into the lungs. At lower than immediately dangerous concentrations, ozone causes headache and dryness of the throat. Some people can distinguish the odor at a few hundredths of a part per million, but this is not usual under smog conditions, since the formaldehyde and acrolein odors generally predominate.

The cheeriest note that Stokinger can come up with is that the continuous exposure to less than fatal doses probably protects the Los Angeles populace from acute attacks of lung edema and hermorrhage. A sinister unanswered question is what is ozone doing *in synergy with other smog components* over a period of years?

Even though laboratory animals can be protected against fatal ozone exposures by pre-conditioning with smaller ozone concentrations, they do not exactly thrive on such pre-conditioning. They age rapidly and generally have an unthrifty look. At such low dosages ozone causes what is called a "radiation-mimotic syndrome"; that is, it acts like radiation poisoning from nuclear-fission sources, and in fact the same anti-radiation drugs, containing sulfur and nitrogen, that protect animals to some extent against radiation are effective in helping them against continued, low-level ozone exposure. There is no doubt that either continued small amounts or periodic larger amounts lead in laboratory animals to chronic fibrosis of the lungs, chronic bronchitis and bronchiolitis. The two processes, development of tolerance to acute attacks and the insidiously developing fibrotic changes in the lungs, go on simultaneously and may be interrelated. It may be necessary to acquire fibrotic lungs to be able to take the red alert concentration (one-half part per million) without gasping out blood into the gutter.

As mentioned above, most of our information on the effects of ozone are obtained through killing laboratory animals. The first spectacular case of acute ozone poisoning in humans was in 1956 among welders who were using a new inert gas-shielded arc process. However, since ozone is encountered at concentrations as high as six parts per million at 80,000 ft. altitude, some work has recently been done by the School of Aviation Medicine of the Air Force using human subjects. This was rather gingerly conducted, and the longest exposure time at concentrations above two parts per million was one hour.

In the six human guinea-pigs it was found that tremendous variation in susceptibility existed, even though all six were young adult males and presumably in good physical condition. In general the sensitivity to ozone was found to be *greater* in men than in the usual laboratory animals. A decrease in lung capacity was noted immediately, but it was only the soft tissues of the respiratory tract that seemed to be attacked. No effects were noted on the blood circulation (pressure or pulse rate) or the conjunctiva of the eyes, but true injury, perhaps permanent in some cases, was observed to the sense of smell. Edema (water on the lungs) became noticeable at the end of one hour.

The Russians have obviously been interested in the toxicity of ozone for some time. Although they have released no information on exposure of men to ozone concentrations of aviation importance, they have found an ominous synergism between sulfuric acid (which can exist in smog aerosols) and ozone in the case of rats. A single exposure to a mixture of ozone and sulfuric acid caused a 70 to 90 per cent fatality rate, much greater than either pollutant used alone in the same concentrations. Pneumonia foci and edema were found in the lungs and, most importantly, plethora was observed in other organs and *in the brain*. This is the first example of air polluted with ozone causing damage to organs remote from the lungs and suggests that when ozone is accompanied by certain other smog ingredients it may have a totally unexpected effect on the cardiovascular system. There is simply not enough known about such synergism to allow anyone to be categorical.

Although sulfuric acid as an ozone synergist is possibly the most spectacular danger that we face in today's smog, it is interesting that hydrogen peroxide is not only a powerful synergist but bestows tolerance in the same way that smaller amounts of ozone do. Moreover, ozone also imparts tolerance to hydrogen peroxide. There are undoubtedly other synergists which we have not yet identified, including stable organic free radicals.

The answer to the question: Did ozone ever kill anyone in Los Angeles? is obviously: We don't know. (The same answer would probably have to be given to a question which to my knowledge nobody has yet dared to raise: Did ozone ever drive anybody crazy in Los Angeles?)

It was feared for some time that ozone along with the nitrogen oxides which are responsible for its existence under smog conditions might constitute an especially wicked combination —a sort of Mac the Knife of smogdom. Stokinger has pretty well deflated this scare, but the nitrogen oxides themselves are not pleasant atmospheric companions. Nitrogen dioxide killed a whole hospital full of people in Cleveland years ago as the result of the spontaneous combustion of stored X-ray films.

Nitrogen dioxide in fact has almost precisely the same effect as ozone—except it requires fifteen times as much to give the same degree of pulmonary edema, hemorrhaging, and death. Fatalities in farmers have resulted from continued exposure to nitrogen dioxide associated with the filling of silos. In man about five hundred parts per million is known to kill instantly. Lower doses result in edema with bronchopneumonia with death in two to ten days; still lower doses in *bronchiolitis fibrosa obliterans* with death in two to three weeks. The American Conference of Governmental Industrial Hygenists has established a tentative threshold limit of five parts per million. (Typically in Los Angeles the NO_2 concentration will reach 0.7 p.p.m. on a smoggy day.) However, Russian investigators report that continued exposure to less than three parts per million has resulted in chronic lung conditions such as the lung disease *emphysema,* which was once known as an occupational hazard of trombone players but has now become quite a popular way to die.

In the case of laboratory animals, Lykova has shown that the effects of long-range exposure of rabbits to low concentrations of nitrogen dioxide include retardation of growth and decrease of red blood corpuscles. In the next chapter we will examine the possibility that, as the result of a new theory of cancer, concentrations of nitrogen dioxide should be kept well below one part per million.

In a strangely overlooked medical journal report, Professor Haagen-Smit has shown that smokers continuously expose themselves to concentrations of nitrogen dioxide that would be regarded as clearly calamitous in smog, and that cigars and pipe tobacco are usually from three to four times worse in this respect than cigarettes. This finding we shall also review later in more detail.

Is there any other sharp knife?

Yes, a smog chemical that Stokinger regards as nearly as dangerous as ozone—ketene. This is an organic substance formed in automotive exhausts which is one of the worst irritants known. As in the case of the poisonous gas phosgene, which it exceeds in toxicity, the lung is the organ affected, with death of severe alveolar epithelial damage resulting in acute congestion, edema, and hemorrhage. The acute symptoms, as with ozone, have little resemblance to the chronic response. Also, as with ozone, small exposures build up tolerance. Rabbits, which are the most resistant laboratory animals to acute high exposure, are the most sensitive to the effects of daily, low-grade (one part per million) exposure.

Are ozone and ketene synergistic buddies? No one has the information. There hasn't been time, but I think it must already be evident to the reader that to the unholy mixture that is modern air pollution we must add the following ingredients: confusion, scientific dismay, frustration, and a sense of helplessness.

chapter 8

CANCER

My lungs so utterly were milked of air . . .

DANTE, *Divine Comedy*

The effect of soots and smokes of various kinds in causing cancer, particularly of the lung and skin, has been known for a long time. A good many decades before the relationship between cigarette smoking and lung cancer was established to the satisfaction of all medical bodies and authorities, with the exception of the notoriously mugwumpish American Medical Association (indeed, the statistical connection is as strong, if not stronger than that between thalidomide and deformed babies), it was known that chimneysweeps were doomed to cancer, if they practiced their profession long enough. In England, insurance companies would rather give an insurance policy to a stunt flyer or an astronaut than to a chimneysweep.

Soots and smokes, whether from the burning of wood, coal, petroleum fuels, rubber, or the Sunday edition of the *New York Times,* contain a family of chemicals known as polycyclic aromatics. Not all the members of this family cause cancer, but the list is formidable. The chemical terms are rather mellifluous. Here are some of them that it is well you don't have in your lungs at this time: benzopyrene, dibenzanthracene, dimethylbenzanthracene (probably the worst of all), benzoperylene, chrysene. All of these are solid materials with high melting points and float around as the finely divided "particulate matter" component of air pollution. The list of known criminal compounds is fragmentary, since only a small per cent of all actual carcinogenic (cancer-producing) materials in soots and smokes have been identified in pure form. Furthermore, there is a growing suspicion that in polluted cities, some compounds that don't belong to the polycyclic family are also active in producing lung cancer or in leading to other kinds of cancer. The situation is at least as complex and confusing as in the case of eye irritation.

There is a frightening gangster relationship between compounds of entirely different types, somewhat similar but not identical to the synergism we have discussed in the previous two chapters. It appears that compound A, which by itself cannot cause cancer, can make the lung tissues more susceptible to compound B, which is the real "hood." This is true also of other lung disease. Animals with scar tissue in the lungs caused by a pulmonary infection are peculiarly likely to contract lung cancer when exposed to the vicious particulate matter.

The human body is well designed against the normal hazards of inhaling gross particulate matter such as bugs and flies and ice crystals. Evolution gave man a beautiful system of cilia in the breathing passages—delicate hair structures to strain out the things that were in the air during paleolithic days and a rhythmic motion of these cilia that works toward ejecting particles that have eluded the nasal sieves. Even now people who breathe scrupulously through their noses rather than go about gaping with their mouths open are partly protected against much of the harmful solids of the atmosphere. It is suspected that the gapers and slack-jawed morons who used to crowd around Hollywood film openings have become extinct (or at least I hope so), either from the fact that Hollywood openings are virtually a thing of the past, or the gapers swallowed too many injurious bugs or too much particulate matter.

The natural selection process of evolution of the species has not had time to develop a defense against *very finely divided* particles, in the form of smokes or smogs, since our paleolithic forefathers were not exposed to such things to the extent that we are. The sinuous fanning motion of the cilia cannot prevent particles below a certain size from getting to the deep internal pulmonary surfaces that are helpless against them.

As we know from the statistical studies of cigarette smoking, lung cancer is a long-time thing. It does not kill human beings overnight or even in a year or so. Perhaps it takes half a million cigarettes—the number a heavy smoker might get through in twenty years or so. If we assume the same degree of delay in response to the carcinogens in polluted cities, Los Angeles has just about reached the point at which deaths from lung cancer caused by air pollution should begin to grow unmistakably.

In the meantime (before the habitual smoker or the habitual inhabitant of a polluted city is given the grace of making his exit by the relatively painless route of lung cancer) he is likely to suffer and die from really rough and agonizing chronic diseases, now believed to be caused by air pollution or smoking, such as emphysema or chronic bronchitis. Bronchitis is more popular in London and emphysema in the United States. In Great Britain, chronic bronchitis, which has been fairly well tied to long exposure to smoke, has become the second most frequent cause of death in men from the ages of forty to fifty-five. Emphysema, where the lung tissues lose their elasticity and the sufferer is in the plight of a man trying to use a bellows made entirely of wood, has probably increased to a much greater extent than the available statistics show, since the average general practitioner, who makes little attempt to keep up with medical knowledge, fails to recognize it. British medical investigators are convinced that a good many people certified in the United

States as dying of coronary heart disease would have been certified in Great Britain as having died of chronic bronchitis or emphysema. This is not unexpected, since when a disease like emphysema is sufficiently advanced a heavy load is thrown on the heart, which must now pump the same volume of blood through far fewer channels available in the greatly reduced air sac lining of the lung. The American Medical Association has done little to rectify the confusion.

Nevertheless the ugly relationship between air pollution and pulmonary disorders is becoming more clearly defined in a world-wide context. A few years ago the so-called "Yokohama asthma" trouble afflicted Air Force personnel in the Tokyo-Yokohama area, and a similar epidemic was reported in New Orleans. Both are now believed to have been associated with air pollution.

People are in special danger from smog who have had a recent experience with Asian influenza. More people in the United States died as a result of Asian flu *after* the 1957 epidemic than *during* it. The 26,000 excess deaths on this account were people with damaged bronchopulmonary structures or chronic heart disease.

It is perhaps impossible to distinguish statistically between diseases, including cancer, caused by air pollution and smoking. Furthermore, smoking *is* air pollution on a minor-league scale. I am an incorrigible smoker myself but have observed, on those infrequent occasions when I have sworn off, that the smoke from other peoples' cigarettes at a cocktail party makes me feel sicker than if it were my own smoke. There was a good deal of sense in great-grandma objecting to the men smoking in the house and that is why great-grandma outlived great-grandpa. The smoke-filled rooms of politicians is one reason why politicians have had short, happy lives.

Nevertheless, in a large smoggy metropolis it is certain that the smokers contribute only a bit of flavor rather than bulk concentration to the emphysema- and cancer-causing components of the air. We are not yet in a position to blame cigarettes for killing throngs of nonsmoking bystanders, including orchids. The automobile can produce more of a variety and a population of carcinogenic materials. In fact, the possibility of cancer from smog has been a great boon to the tobacco industry and its hard-pressed public relations people, because it gives them a somewhat precarious whipping-boy. A story that has been told by them in almost infinite variation, so often that it seems to be a whole encyclopedia of stories, is the one about the English colonizers who moved to New Zealand. They came from urban cockney stock, inveterate smokers all, but they and their children, who smoked even more but were raised in the pure air that surrounds New Zealand sheepherders, never had any trouble with lung cancer or even emphysema or bronchitis. Although these statistics have been wrung out to a somewhat suspicious degree of dryness, there is probably a core of fact in them.

A careful survey of English cigarette smokers living in rural and urban environments has shown that the rural smoker has a little better chance of survival. Moreover, some information recently released by the Sloan-Kettering Institute is very instructive. If you collect the solid material from an automobile exhaust and purify it to the extent that you presumably isolate the een-compounds, and do the same thing with cigarette smoke, you find that the purified compounds from exhaust smoke are twice as likely to cause skin cancer in mice as those from cigarettes. This is one of those facts that the non-medically sophisticated can easily respond to with their "So what?" "What does a skin tumor on a mouse have to do with my lungs?"

Of necessity, the major body of our data on the carcinogenic behavior of either smog or cigarette smoke is based on laboratory animals. Unless we suddenly revert to Hitlerian morality, we cannot immerse human beings in smog chambers for years at a time until we find that they are finally unable to breathe. Skin cancer in mice is a fast-developing thing, easy to measure and to analyze statistically, and there is some degree of assurance at least that it correlates with lung cancer in mice, which involves a difficult smog experiment, since the animal is likely to die first of something else—old age, for example. Furthermore, there is some degree of correlation, as we have seen, between mice and men in the case of ozone. The experimental findings with mice have in a general way been confirmed by experiments with hamsters, rabbits, dogs, guinea pigs, rats, monkeys, even birds and frogs. There are some disturbing things about the skin tumor results. For example, when tumor-forming agents are rubbed on a mouse's back, the mouse may develop cancer of the breasts. When mice are exposed to known carcinogens by skin contact, injection in the blood or oral injection, they are likely to develop lung cancer. These are examples of what the medical investigators call "remote action." Other studies have shown that a single application to the skin of an amount of carcinogen inadequate to induce a tumor produces nevertheless a *latent tumor change*. Skin so treated will develop tumors if exposed later to another chemical that itself is not carcinogenic. This is the reverse of the team of "finger man plus hood" mentioned previously, and such combinations make the smog doctor's life very complicated. Establishing a realistic tolerance level in city atmospheres to specific dangerous materials becomes almost impossible.

Chemicals coming out of exhaust pipes are not the only suspicious ones. Finely powdered asphalt and rubber are good sources of carcinogens, since when particles of these materials are dispersed in the air they can be converted by photochemical oxidation to give chemicals that cause cancer. Not long ago somebody made the front pages by suggesting that the new synthetic rubbers for tires would help cure the smog evil because the greater resistance of such tires to abrasive wear would free the atmosphere made foul by teen-agers squealing their jalopies around corners. Although this is a bit far-fetched, one cannot overlook another almost limitless source of cancer from the atmosphere. This is from "free radicals."

Chemists apply this term to compounds whose structure is such that they have at least one "unpaired electron"—that is, one electron which is not properly busy in teaming up with other electrons in the job of keeping the molecule in one piece. A free radical is like a school bus with one wild kid sticking himself three feet out the window—his head is likely to get knocked off, and similarly an unpaired electron is more than likely to get into all kinds of mischief. It is spoiling to stick its head into the business of other molecules.

In a test tube free radicals are not likely to survive very long, because they either react with each other (two unpaired electrons on separate molecules uniting in the marriage that they so desperately need) or they will react with normal, well-behaved molecules, pulling out a hydrogen atom, for example, to satisfy their electron hunger, leaving the other molecule now in a free radical state; this molecule will then in turn go chasing after electrons, yank them from still other molecules and this rat-race continues, becoming what is known as a "chain reaction." One free radical can then cause a tremendous chemical tumult, which in fact is the way things burn. Flaming combustion is a "branched chain" free radical process. However, the free radicals involved in combustion are small, exceedingly hysterical and could not last long in any atmosphere. This is not true of certain other free radicals. One must remember that even in the foulest air the concentration of all molecules, except nitrogen, oxygen, argon, and carbon dioxide, is measured in parts per million. One of chemistry's foundations is the "law of mass action" that says a compound reacts at a rate proportional to its concentration. Thus at the dilutions in which air pollutants exist on even the smoggiest day, they will not react to destroy themselves as fast as in concentrations commonly used in the laboratory.

Two relatively new things are now believed about free radicals: first, they can survive for periods of hours in the atmosphere and second, they have something to do with cancer. These beliefs are not necessarily both shared at the same time by respective experts in the fields of free radical chemistry and medicine. The Warburg theory of cancer causation by free radicals involves too complicated a parcel of biochemistry to be examined in detail here, but suffice to say that it fits in curiously well with what we know about such cancer diseases as leukemia stimulated by nuclear radiation.

We have mentioned that certain smog agents exert a "radiation-mimotic" effect; they imitate the effects of radiation. If it is true, as some suspect, that a significant proportion of not only radiation-caused cancers but all cancers may be associated with the action of free radicals in the human body, then we must have another and even fiercer look at free radicals that float around a smoggy city.

Brilliant research work with mice which broadened considerably the scope of atmospheric carcinogenic studies has been done by Kotin and his associates of the University of Southern California. Not only do they conclude that free radicals can cause neoplastic growth but a whole disparate family of chemical compounds previously believed to be blameless as far as cancer is concerned is now under suspicion—including epoxides, peracids, aldehydes, peroxides, ozonides, and ketenes.

One of the most depressing aspects of Kotin's findings is that many of the smog compounds, even in amounts incapable of causing cancer, have an unfavorable effect on the reproduction of mice and the survival of offspring. This is an interesting corroboration of observations made many years ago of the reduced fecundity of ewes exposed to urban smoke in England. Such smoke has also been connected with the incidence of human cancer of the stomach and intestines.

Kotin's work has aroused ire among many people, especially doctors on the staffs of large petroleum and automobile companies. Such doctors are paid to believe only such notions as are favorable to the interests of the companies who hire them, and therefore the name of Kotin is about as popular among such men as the name of Karl Marx. In my experience the opinions of such doctors concerning air pollution are completely worthless. I have caught them in errors of scientific fact that even a high-school chemistry student would be ashamed of.

Some of the more sophisticated hired defenders of the interests of smog-makers have, however, taken a different approach. This is to publish an impressively documented paper, proving that Poison Z is not produced in automotive exhausts, and that Poison Z in fact disappears prudently when the automotive traffic is heaviest. Thus a General Motors chemist has shown elaborately that benzopyrene cannot be detected in significant amounts in exhaust smoke. Even if this were true (and the observations of Kotin and of others contradict it) the implication that exhaust smoke therefore does not contribute to danger from cancer is like deciding that a man is not a victim of poison because no arsenic can be found in him.

We are beyond the comfortably simple stage of arsenic and even the polycyclics with names rhyming with "Irene." The free radical theory of cancer has added a new dimension to the smog problem, and even if free radicals are ultimately found not the worst offenders in smog-activated cancer, their presence in the atmosphere and their great chemical activity makes one fear they must be up to no good. Free radicals can be detected by a technique known as "electron spin resonance," and it is certain that from now on the "ESR" spectrometer will be a routine part of the modern smogster's equipment.

Although the free radical population that is most dangerous probably consists of large, normally solid compounds of Irene's family, but with a missing hydrogen atom and an unpaired electron residing somewhere in the structure, one must call attention to the fact that in the technical sense of the definition, the nitrogen oxides are also free radicals. They have unpaired electrons. Thus their special danger may be related less to their murderous attack in large concentrations, with results similar to those of ozone in amounts over the red alert limit, but to their long-term, low-concentration, cumulative threat as carcinogens. We have mentioned in the last chapter Haagen-Smit's extraordinary discovery that nitrogen dioxide from tobacco smoking can far exceed the amounts regarded as likely to be fatal to human beings, if the human beings were put in a cage and made to breathe such amounts in the available air. One cannot suspect Haagen-Smit's data since, as an analyst in this sort of thing, his record is absolutely impeccable. Can it be that in this case we have a case of "negative synergism"? Does some other common constituent of tobacco smoke, perhaps even the polycyclic tars, neutralize the nitrogen oxides?

Haagen-Smit shows a tremendously wide variation from one tobacco to another, but generally it is the tobacco made for pipes and cigars that gives the highest nitrogen oxide level. Since little or no nitrogen fixation process can take place at low pressures and temperatures of tobacco smoking, the nitrogen oxides are formed from the burning of organic nitrogen in the tobacco, probably from agricultural sprays, urea-type fertilizers or from proteins present in the natural tobacco in varying degree.

chapter 9

. . . AND MADNESS?

There is a pleasure sure
In being mad which none but madmen know.

DRYDEN, *The Spanish Friar*

Some years ago a hot-springs retreat in Southern California which was at that time just outside the wind roses that carried smog from the center of the automobile traffic (from the "eye" of the hurricane, so to speak) towards Disneyland and towards Riverside, a gabby matron announced to everybody who would listen to her that the Los Angeles smog had caused her to have a complete nervous breakdown. Under doctor's orders, she was going to stay right here just outside the tentacles of the smog and recover her mental equilibrium. This evoked behind her back mild guffaws, especially since it was her habit to consume two bottles of Muscatel and a bottle of apricot brandy every day—a rather high ration even for this place which specialized in gently loony rich alcoholics.

Were the guffaws justified? Is it possible that automotive smog can cause neurosis? Here I don't refer to people being "driven to distraction" or perhaps "driven to drink" by eye-irritation and the like, but to the possibility that there are ingredients in smog that might specifically affect the brain.

There is absolutely no concrete information on this matter, and as far as I know, nobody has ever considered it seriously or has any plans to study the problem, even from a statistical viewpoint. This chapter will therefore be short, since it will

[112]

consist mainly of speculation.

We do have the apparently impeccable Russian finding that sulfuric aerosols in combination with ozone can cause swelling of brain tissue in rats. Such studies, however, were not accompanied by any observations of the behavior of the rats before they died. A rat trying desperately to breath through a hemorrhaging lung is above all a dying rat and is only incidentally neurotic or psychotic, as perhaps is every animal in the final stages of suffocation. Peculiar behavior has been noted in laboratory animals exposed to less than lethal concentrations of smog chemicals, but laboratory animals are somewhat impatient in unwholesome atmospheres and nobody has ascertained whether over a protracted period of smog they would start reaching for the bottle and become rodent winos.

If we are dealing with possible mental deterioration as a result of smog, it is probably a long-term deterioration, like cancer of the lung. Unfortunately there is nothing in the open scientific literature about extended effects of exposure of animals, including man, to chemicals designed to make an enemy temporarily so silly that he cannot fight. There is a proliferating *classified* literature, since lysergic acid derivatives and other compounds receive continued attention from the Chemical Warfare Branch of the Army; in fact, all major military powers, and some minor ones, devote a good deal of time and money to the synthesis and biological testing of chemicals for driving entire populations of their enemies mad rather than killing them. The objective is to provoke temporary insanity or mental helplessness rather than to achieve a permanent mass psychosis, since it would be nearly as embarrassing to deal with a conquered country of hopeless lunatics, as it would be to clean up occupied territory inhabited only by the dead. (The much publicized "Nerve Gas" which was invented by the German chemist

[113]

Schrader during World War II and which is held in large supply by both the United States and Russia does not belong in this category. It is a killer rather than a goof-maker and its structural similarity to many phosphorus-containing pesticides has caused justifiable concern to Rachel Carson and others.)

In recent military experimentation consequently the chemicals that cause cumulative and irreversible brain deterioration are regarded as failures, and their effects are not further pursued but they are put on the shelf for future reference.

It can be said without violation of military security that some of these chemicals belong to a *family* of compounds that has been isolated in small amounts from the "particulate-matter" fraction of Los Angeles smog samples.

After all, this should not be surprising to an organic chemist. If one combines the hydrocarbons from automotive exhausts with nitrogen (and chlorine, bromine, phosphorus, and boron from fuel additives), oxygen and sulfur in a gaseous wilderness shot through with strong sunlight, one would expect to come out with at least traces of practically every imaginable chemical compound except those containing exotic metal atoms. The question is not whether brain-damaging chemicals exist in smog, but to what average extent they exist, and whether this average extent is dangerous to people's brains and behavior.

There is no information available on this question, and I doubt whether anyone in the foreseeable future will attempt to develop it. This is a subject that is so delicate because of its military security aspects on the one hand and its medical-political ramifications on the other, that even such fearless smogsters as Kokinger and Kotin might hesitate to tackle it full-tilt.

There is, however, another, at first glance rather jolly, possibility of mental effects from smog which may be temporary or may not, and if it can be demonstrated more scientifically than it has been so far, might conceivably point a way towards temporarily increasing rather than lowering mental acuity. This is concerned with *ions*. These are not even chemical blood-brothers to the free radicals whose behavior we examined with disapproval and some forebodings in the last chapter. Ions are electrically charged chemical species. They can be detected in flames but normally are not seen strolling around the air of a city, since they combine rapidly, the positive ions with the negative ones, and are readily discharged by contact with various surfaces. However, they are definitely more numerous in atmospheres polluted with automotive exhausts. Scientists of the Swedish Royal Institute of Technology have shown that the exhaust-gas cloud contains an astonishing population of ions, which decreases rapidly with distance from the exhaust pipe. The ions seem to be mainly associated with smoke particles and their number can be increased by the presence of gasoline additives.

Ions in the air are not caused only by automobiles or even only by combustion, but have always been with us to some extent because of the ionizing effect of natural radioactivity in the soil and cosmic rays. The ion population is, of course, increased by radioactive fall-out from nuclear explosions. Generally, however, some air pollution in the form of particulate matter is necessary to have ions that last very long. The most stable ions are the large ones associated with carbon particles, and measurements show that in the air of large cities they are more prevalent than in the country, and they are favored by sunny days. The concentration of small ions is higher in summer, highest in the early morning and lowest in the early afternoon. At low altitudes the concentration of small positive ions is greater than that of small negative ions because of the mobilizing effect on the latter of the earth's magnetic field.

Ions can be produced in air deliberately by electrical discharge methods and there has been a large amount of medical study associated with the effect of ions on such activities as the ciliary motion in the respiratory tract, stimulation of mucous membranes, blood pressure, convalescence time, basal metabolism, endocrine gland productivity, etc., but the most interesting results have been those connected with the effect of ions on the nervous system—on pain intensity and electric encephalograms ("brain waves"). Ionized air has been found to reduce the pain from burns, and negative ions seem occasionally to exert a general tranquilizing effect.

Starting with the early 1930's almost a cult of air-ion therapy took hold in European clinics. One went to an ion-therapy clinic for vague malaises, including chronic rheumatism and melancholia. A slight odor of quackery attached itself to such clinics and still does. (It has always been possible to attract suckers to anything by use of the word *electricity*.)

Nevertheless there are some recent findings by applied psychologists that ionized air may not only make people feel better but make them function more brightly. It has been proposed to pipe ionized air into offices to keep the staff from taking coffee-breaks every half-hour. Unfortunately the more carefully controlled tests do not seem to come out the same way every time. In some cases ionized air seems to make people restless rather than tranquil, and careless rather than alert.

It seems probable that a rather narrow band of tolerance for ions exists, and that above the concentration associated with pleasant and useful effects, an urban population exposed to high amounts of ions, especially the heavy ions met with in smog rather than the light ions produced artificially, may react in a generally mischievous way. Is this what causes Los Angeles and Tokyo occasionally to indulge in very reckless mass escapades?

In the bad smog December of 1955 practically all of Los Angeles apparently decided to get drunk and get arrested for reckless driving on Christmas Eve. No such Christmas Eve had been seen in a large city before. The jails filled up with otherwise respectable people. Los Angeles is not a steadily heavy-drinking city; at least it is not in the same class with definitely alcoholic cities such as San Francisco and Washington, D.C., but such outbreaks of dangerous mass silliness are not uncommon there. Perhaps there should be an ion Red Alert as well as one for ozone.

F. Scott Fitzgerald wrote a story about a man's return to a city where he had been many times before and where he had, in fact, lived briefly. The city seemed strange to him. There was an unfamiliar sharpness of outline, a nagging intensity of sounds, a difference in the weight of the air. Suddenly he realized that this was the only time he had been cold sober in this city. It was he, not the city, that was changed.

The ions of smog may in Los Angeles cast a spell on its inhabitants like the psychic veil of alcohol. If the ions are discharged, perhaps the inhabitants may be more gentle, less prone to general attacks of silliness and may enjoy their sparkling San Gabriel mountains and live at ease in their canyons rather than despoiling them. They may even get over their senseless generalized preoccupation with moving dirt. The symbol of Los Angeles is not so much the automobile or the surf rider as it is the giant 40 mile-per-hour Le Tourneau dirt-mover that levels gracious little hills in the wink of a weekend to make room for parking lots and pizza huts. This obsession with gouging hills away and moving dirt from one spot to another has even inspired some of the restless great brains of the metropolis to suggest what is unquestionably the most grandiose and most absurd smog-cure ever dreamed of—cutting great channels in the mountains to let the smog blow out into the Mojave desert.

chapter 10

WHAT IS BEING DONE

The futile dialogue of mode . . .
WATSON, The Things that Are More Excellent

The problem of air pollution, especially the Los Angeles situation and the gradually awakening awareness to the fact that Los Angeles is a portent rather than merely an unlucky town with too many automobiles, has made some good jobs available for people who might otherwise have become small-town M.D.'s, analytical chemists for tuna-packers, or shoe clerks. A majority of all air-pollution engineers, chemists, and administrators in the country are located in Los Angeles. In addition to the staffs that work for such agencies as the California Motor Vehicle Pollution Control Board, the L.A. County Air Pollution Control District (lately transferred to the authority of the former), the U. S. Public Health Service, and such institutions as the Robert Taft Sanitary Engineering Center in Cincinnati, there are numerous university investigators who spend full time on smog problems. A group at the University of California, Riverside, is very active as are scientific groups at Berkeley, Stanford, UCLA, Cal Tech and the University of Southern California.

In local control programs over the whole United States there are a total of about one thousand people directly on payrolls, about 500 of them reporting to the L.A. County Air Pollution Control District.

In spite of the beehive air of things being accomplished and the happy prospects of smog being legislated out of existence, it is nevertheless quite probable that the measures proposed to alleviate the automotive smog problem may actually make it worse. For example, there is not enough known about smog chemistry to say for certain whether or not the compulsory use of catalytic mufflers or afterburners on cars for removing a large proportion of the hydrocarbons from gasoline from the atmosphere, will result in a corresponding increase of nitrogen dioxide and perhaps start killing people outright.

Professor Emeritus Philip Leighton of Stanford, who has written a learned book on the photochemistry of air pollution, believes that the selective removal of hydrocarbons from exhaust may bring about a definitely hazardous condition because of the fact that the nitrogen oxides would then disappear more slowly because they would have fewer things to react with. Although this point of view is disputed by savants at the University of California at Riverside, the very fact that there should be such a dispute indicates that Los Angeles County and the State of California are rushing into applications of the police power to enforce regulations in an area where nobody agrees about the facts involved.

It is possible to build up a somewhat similar case in regard to that pathetic "fix"—the cigarette filter. These filters do not remove the very finely divided particles of aerosols or smoke, they take out only the relatively coarse particles. In the absence of the coarse particles, the smaller ones are less likely to nucleate on the large ones during passage through the respiratory tract, and thus the net result is probably simply a change in size distribution with actually a greater concentration of active particulate matter getting into the lungs. The filter-tip cigarette advertisements blossom all over with figures on percentages of "tar" and nicotine removed, but there are no reliable figures on the comparative clinical effects of smoke inhaled from filter-tip and ordinary cigarettes nor even on the effect of particle-size distribution. The only sure fix would be a chemical-absorbing filter and this would give the smoker simply a mouthful of cold nitrogen. It would be about as exciting as eating pure snow instead of ice cream.

When the Los Angeles County Air Pollution Control laboratory was established in 1950, the automobile was not yet thoroughly identified as chief villain. A lot of solid work was done by this authority in cleaning up the fringe sources of pollution, such as getting the oil refineries to bottle up their own sulfurous fume emissions, setting limits on the sulfur content of heavy fuels, putting a stop to backyard trash-burning, policing dry-cleaning establishments and, with the help of such consultants as Professor Haagan-Smit, teaching industrial engineers how to run boiler plants, power-generating units and other large fuel-burning installations so that a minimum of nitrogen oxides would be formed.

It is true that all this did not to the slightest perceptible degree prevent smog. The smog events continued, the same or worse in both frequency and intensity, but such activities served the purpose at least of making the automobile clearly the culprit. Thus in the past few years the delousing of the internal combustion engine has been the main objective of the Los Angeles County and the state smog authorities.

This has turned out to be a problem essentially about a hundred times as difficult as flying a man to the moon. The easy things have been done. Emission of smogging materials from the crankcase of automobiles and trucks has been discouraged by the compulsory uses of vents from the crankcase leading back to the engine. The Control Board in September, 1963, set final regulations for enforcing two state laws regarding such crankcase devices in used cars and trucks, and new cars sold in California had already been equipped with back-venting systems in 1961 and 1962.

The rather hopeful assumption is that the gases that blow by the cylinders into the crankcase amount to as much as thirty per cent of the total smog-forming emission from an automotive vehicle. Thus if these gases are sucked back into the engine and burned again, the theory is that California air will be 30 per cent less smoggy. The 30 per cent figure is either extremely optimistic or pessimistic, depending on the way you look at it. If 30 per cent of the total exhaust comes from the crankcase, the automobiles and trucks in California are in awful shape and need new compression rings.

The truth is that the 30 per cent figure represents one of these magic numbers, pulled out of the air, like "26 per cent fewer dental cavities." Furthermore, there is some as yet undefined amount of engine deterioration caused by feeding dirty air back to it. The engine itself doesn't like smog. One of the troubles in traffic-choked freeways is that a car breathes in the exhaust from the car in front of it. Although air cleaners are standard equipment on modern cars, these are even less ideally efficient in operation than a filter-tip on a cigarette. Intake-valve sticking and probably spark-plug fouling can result from feeding an automobile air containing chemical compounds that form gummy deposits. Thus with the crankcase blow-by feedback system we may be in for an epidemic of misfiring engines, which could create almost as much smog as it is hoped to remove.

At least, we can say the equipping of the three million new cars with factory-installed crankcase vent devices that were sold in California in the years from 1961 through 1963 did not put a dent in smog virulence. The worst smog in five years hit Los Angeles in the second week of September, 1963.

Another easy thing to do was to require that motor fuel sold in California contain no more than a certain amount of olefin hydrocarbons. These regulations were based on two theories, both of which were unsound. One was that the amount of olefins in the atmosphere completely determines the amount of the most noxious smog constituents. Although it is pretty well proved that certain olefins react more quickly than other exhaust compounds to form eye-irritants, this is about all that *can* be said. As we have mentioned before, even in the case of eye irritation the presence of olefins in the atmosphere seems to determine only whether your eyes hurt in the morning or the afternoon.

The second fallacy is that the olefin content of the exhaust directly reflects the olefin content of the original gasoline. This is true only when the engine is operating with no burning at all. As has been mentioned in Chapter 7, the engine is an artful producer of olefins from the most bland and innocuous of fuels; in fact there are processes for commercially producing certain olefins (which are valuable in making synthetic rubber) by partial oxidation of normal hydrocarbons. The main effect of the olefin regulations has been to make it more expensive to make gasoline in California. This is because the key process in most gasoline-producing refineries the world over is catalytic "cracking," whereby heavier oils are broken up into high-octane light fuels and a rather large proportion of the light fuels contain olefins. We can say of the olefin regulations only that they gave the public the comforting idea that decisions were being made and enforced.

This regulation and the crankcase-vent laws, however, were only preliminaries to the Great Leap. This is compulsory use of catalytic or other auxiliary devices on car and truck mufflers to burn everything in the exhaust gases that will burn. The selection of an approved device is based on engine tests in which the treated exhaust must contain less than 1.5 per cent carbon monoxide and less than 275 parts per million of hydrocarbons. The race to qualify such a device (and two gadgets from different manufacturers had to be approved one year before the law took effect) early narrowed down to seven companies, five with catalyst systems and two in which extra air is pumped into the muffler to produce an actual flame.

This is a tough assignment. It is not difficult to run an engine steadily and take out the hydrocarbons, the carbon monoxide and perhaps even the nitrogen oxides, but automobile engines in a big city don't run steadily; they run like drunken witches, with stops, starts, idling, accelerations, decelerations, huffs and puffs, screeching stops and sliding glides. In the case of the catalytic system, nothing happens at all until the catalyst has warmed up, and it then may overheat or it may be poisoned by various compounds from the engine. The direct-flame approach has even more bugs, and it puts a frightening amount of heat in the back area of the car near the gasoline tank. People are uncomfortable about building a fire under a tank of gasoline.

All the candidate devices must pass a 10,000-mile endurance test. The manufacturer must pay $5000 for a test on one vehicle, and "Step One" in the series of approval tests calls for testing twenty-four vehicles. Some of the possible competitors are catalyst manufacturing or specialized automotive hardware companies that don't like to spend that kind of money. Enthusiasm for the Great Leap has notably dwindled among the small companies. They originally saw a chance for a jackpot, since at least nineteen other states have gone on record as ready to follow California's lead, and Senator Edward Long of Missouri introduced a bill in Congress to require that all automobiles sold in the U.S. be equipped with anti-smog devices.

As of early summer, 1964, the California State Motor Vehicle

Pollution Board had certified four exhaust control devices for *new* cars. This automatically triggered a California law that makes it compulsory for all 1966 and later-model cars and pickup trucks sold in the state to have exhaust control devices —either one of these four or any other system certified from now on.

The four that have so far been blessed are a direct-flame afterburner developed by American Machine and Foundry Company under a license from Chromalloy Corp. and three catalytic units: Arvin Industries–Universal Oil Products; W. R. Grace Co.–Norris Thermador; and Walker Manufacturing Co.–American Cyanamid. (Observe that these combinations consist for the most part of hardware companies backed up by chemical concerns.)

This becomes Act I of a rather mean but explosive farce.

Let us first examine the significance of the technical approvals. The tests that have been "passed" were all run by sophisticated test managers under controlled conditions. The results of such a "white coat" type of test unfortunately very seldom bear much relation to random statistical results which would be obtained by letting the public try the device out in relatively large numbers. The people who make additive chemicals for lubricating oils or motor fuels, for example, would not dream of accepting the kind of test results that have given the four successful devices an official O.K., costly as they were. The automobile manufacturers, the oil company chemists, and even the more worldly of the smog savants know this very well. The data in hand would justify only putting the four devices to a statistically meaningful examination in hundreds of cars before deciding whether any substantial advance in automotive smog prevention had truly been achieved.

What the State Motor Vehicle Pollution Control Board has

in mind is to make the actual customer bear the burden of the true test in the case of thousands of 1966 model cars and trucks. Since new vehicles will amount to less than ten per cent of the cars on the road in California, there will be no way of determining the actual effect of the law until a much larger percentage of exhaust-device-equipped vehicles hit the road. The cost of putting devices on used cars is much greater than on factory models, and this move can be dismissed at the present time as a purely romantic notion, although the chairman of the pollution board has suggested that the American Machine and Foundry flame afterburner be at least certified for 1962 and later models, provided that one or more other devices are also found suitable for used cars.

Perhaps by 1970 one should be expected to judge whether the mass equipment is successful or not. By that time it is quite likely that attention will have been re-focused on Professor Leighton's favorite smog poison, nitrogen dioxide, the concentration of which in the California atmosphere may have reached a whiskey-brown level. They may pile smog device upon smog device until the driving public hollers that it would rather be poisoned than broke.

The farcical element for the potential manufacturers of the present devices is that, except for Chrysler Corp., the auto industry, as represented by the Automobile Manufacturers Association, has brushed off the whole solemn device-test scheme in California with the collective statement that starting with 1966 models, cars for California will be taken care of by the car manufacturers themselves on their own assembly lines. What this means is open to some question.

It has been taken by some to signify that all manufacturers will accept some such simple, cheap, and highly dubious system as the "ManAirOx" (manifold air oxidation), in which air is pumped into the exhaust gas manifold and aimed at the exhaust valves in the hope that it may be hot enough at such locations to burn up exhausting unburned or partly burned fuel and carbon monoxide, or it may involve the Chrysler concept of the "Clean Air Package" (basic changes in the engine operation to alter valve and ignition timing and carburetor modifications to achieve more complete combustion) or it may be a combination of both systems. Actually it has not been demonstrated as of this writing that either "ManAirOx" or the Chrysler system will do the job, as defined by the Control Board. What *is* quite certain are the following facts:

1. General Motor's "ManAirOx" system and a similar system developed by Ford will not reduce carbon monoxide to the required levels.

2. The Chrysler system will do a better job than exhaust manifold air-injection on carbon monoxide but a poorer job on cleaning up hydrocarbons.

3. The combination of both systems may skin by, on a lenient reading of the rules, but the hydrocarbons that do escape from the exhaust will be more active smog-wise (because of the fast-idle chemical conditions in the Chrysler spark and carburetor adjustments and the low-pressure partial oxidation reactions in the exhaust manifold device).

4. A definitely higher percentage of nitrogen oxides will be added to the atmosphere.

Whatever the factory-installed 1966 fixes turn out to be, they are not going to be good news for the potential device manufacturers. They would have undergone all the agony and the expense of research and testing for a one-year market. They can only hope to get a second-hand car outlet, as the law moves into this area, and here the situation is fairly hopeless.

Nor are the California air pollution authorities very pleased with the Automobile Manufacturers Association stand. With some justifications they claim that Detroit has not kept them informed, and one can wonder whether, in the present phase of a problem of such monstrous complexity, Detroit itself is informed. In a recent hearing the chairman of the Automobile Manufacturers Association's Vehicle Combustion Product Committee said that he questions the future importance of controlling nitrogen oxide emissions—a point that has been brought up for consideration in regard to a possible future second wave of exhaust specifications, which might also lower the allowable concentration of unburned fuel and CO. This is the almost too completely predictable statement. Since the quick-and-dirty "ManAirOx" fix or the Chrysler fix will not remove nitrogen oxides, nitrogen oxides cannot be of any importance. (The Chrysler fix in fact should definitely result in *more* nitrogen oxides and the Chrysler fix is necessarily included with "ManAirOx.")

Let us once again look into their nitrogen oxide problem from a "clinico-political" standpoint. Although it has become fashionable for Detroit-polarized bodies such as the AMA (although I refer to the Automobile Manufacturers Association, the same is disgracefully true of another AMA, the American Medical Association) to pooh-pooh the danger of nitrogen dioxide in a fashion somewhat parallel to the pooh-poohing of chronic carbon monoxide poisoning (cf. Chapter 4), one need only review Stokinger's findings (cf. Chapter 7) and the Cleveland Clinic Hospital catastrophe to disabuse oneself of a feeling of indifference towards this noxious little free-radical molecule.

Actually this horrifying accident in Cleveland should have been included in the air-pollution disaster story, since it not only involved at a lethal level our enemy nitrogen dioxide but killed more people than the combined victims in the incidents of the Meuse Valley, Donora, and Poza Rica.

On May 15, 1929, the x-ray films stored too near a steam pipe in the basement of the Cleveland Clinic Hospital exploded and a general fire started. At that time nitrocellulose was used for the manufacture of such films, and the decomposition products were mainly nitrogen dioxide (although the next day's newspaper headlines idiotically identified the poison as bromine). The "whiskey-brown" fumes billowed up through the three floors of the hospital and killed one hundred and twenty-five people, mostly in their beds. Victims were carried out foaming green at the mouth. However, the most disturbing aspect of the disaster was the after-effects in the case of those who didn't have to be carried out.

A girl stenographer fled the fumes and jumped out a ground-floor window of the hospital. She ran to her home a few blocks away and, since she had been exposed only to a sniff or two of the poison gas, she considered herself safe. She was persuaded, however, two days later to go to her doctor for a check-up. In the doctor's office, talking and laughing with friends, she suddenly collapsed and died.

A husky ex-football player, convalescent from a tonsillectomy, also jumped out a window, having been exposed minimally to the fumes. The next day he drove his car a hundred and fifty miles on business. While transacting his affairs, he suddenly sat down in an office chair, slid off the chair in convulsions and died.

There were other borderline cases of delayed deaths from partial exposure to the whiskey-brown gas. Although the toxicology of nitrogen dioxide was not very well understood in 1929, the post-mortems indicated peculiar lung corrosion along with some poorly defined damage to the sympathetic nervous system.

If, as in the case of carbon monoxide, it is allowable to draw a parallel between the clinical effects of short-time exposure to a medium amount of toxic gas and constant exposure to a small amount, Professor Leighton is right, and we are all headed for real trouble.

In its plan for stricter controls by 1970, the California Board had wanted to include a nitrogen oxide specification number for the first time, but no such number appears in the neatly mimeographed account of the "1970 Plan." It proposes to reduce the allowable hydrocarbon content of exhaust gas from 275 to 180 parts per million and the allowable carbon monoxide concentration from one and a half per cent to one per cent, but the only mention of nitrogen oxides is a sort of pious resolution which, in effect, says the Board doesn't like nitrogen oxides.

There is an interesting reason for this strange behavior. The Attorney General of the State of California had advised that to include a restriction on nitrogen oxides without "implementation" would "prejudice" the legality of the new restrictions on hydrocarbons and carbon monoxide. "Implementation" in this context was a lawyer's word for the fact that there was no device or method available for meeting a nitrogen oxide specification.

Now, let us examine the kind of vicious circle we get caught up in. Recently a story for a national magazine on the nitrogen oxide situation was turned down on the grounds that "Detroit is fully aware of the nitrogen oxides situation and will do something about it when it is *required* [by law]." (This magazine supports itself to a large extent on full-page or multi-page automobile advertisements and evidently had made a quick-call to Detroit in regard to the suitability of the article in question.

It has become a bold magazine in recent years, attacking such institutions as Alimony, Alcoholics Anonymous and football coaches, but it is not *that* bold!)

Thus we have the agonizingly absurd situation of the smog authorities refusing to recommend a law to limit the emissions of a known toxic gas, because there is no commercially established method for coping with the gas, and the automobile companies refusing to develop such a method because there is no law requiring them to do so.

That is the nitrogen oxide situation as of the autumn of 1964.

Let us go back to the 1966 model automobile as promised for California and expected not long afterward for the rest of the country. The Chrysler Clean Air Package, although based on the commendable principle of policing and tuning up the engine so that it always runs with a minimum of unburned fuel or CO in the exhaust, is simply not a practical package in a naughty world. The lack of practicality is indicated by the fact that early test failures in attempting to pass the California test requirements were blamed on "adjustment changes made by unauthorized persons." Current engines under test in Chrysler's attempt in the official California procedure to get a pass are sealed.

The Clean Air Package in effect sets a tightrope for a driver to walk. In stepping up the engine speed for idling, the engine runs so lean under certain conditions that the average driver would be in an almost continuous state of exasperation. The engine would be "killed" so often, with the unskilled manipulation that must be expected, that it is actually conceivable, because of increased number of start-ups per car trip, that in mass practice more smog ingredients would be released than before.

Los Angeles County understandably sympathizes with Chrysler, gives it "A for Effort" for its participation in the smog test derby, and in December, 1963, the L.A. County Board of Supervisors directed its purchasing agent to purchase only those cars that emit less than 300 p.p.m. exhaust hydrocarbons (more than the State Board specifications but an impressive improvement over no specifications), knowing full well that the only cars that could pretend to meet this requirement were Chrysler-made ones equipped with the Clean Air Package. This has resulted in subsequent purchase by the county of some 200 Chrysler-made cars and only four from other companies (for special secret work). Thus the supervisors applied a weapon they thought the industry understands best. When a recent purchase of 83 cars went to a Chrysler products dealer whose bid was six thousand dollars higher than the lowest one, other bidders protested. The supervisors replied, in effect, "Take your squawks back to Detroit."

If all this sounds confusing, it is. We have California State and Los Angeles County authorities working feverishly to get some sort of legal control going on the basis of fundamentally unpromising, possibly dangerous techniques, and we have Detroit turning up its nose, for the most part, but in the meantime pulling the rug from under the device manufacturers. The eyes of the rest of the country (especially the eyes of cities which have exceeded L.A. in recent smog episodes, including Cincinnati and St. Louis) are trying to focus on this fantastically raddled picture. What they have seen so far is not edifying.

Perhaps some of the unmistakable discouragement that now pervades the scene is the growing realization that the Great Leap is more than likely to be a Great Flop.

There is not much margin of profit in sight, even if the device manufacturers have still the used car market to exploit.

Consider the simple economics of a truly technically successful muffler, assuming one can be developed to remove *all* the smog-forming chemicals, including the nitrogen oxides. Realistically it will cost over $150 and will require the attention of expert maintenance mechanics. This is as much as the sales price of hundreds of thousands of jalopies in Los Angeles and there are not enough garage mechanics of any degree of expertise whatever in the whole state of California to do the installation, let alone the maintenance job.

A law that makes it necessary for everybody to pay $150 or more for a piece of hardware he doesn't understand nor knows how to fix is almost *ipso facto* an unenforceable law. There are not enough jails in the country or enough policemen or enough testers or enough garages or enough judges or politicians to make the law stand up.

There are those who will quarrel with my $150 figure for a truly effective catalytic muffler. I have been associated with catalysts all my working life and am personally convinced that a really effective anti-smog catalyst apparatus will cost considerably more than this. I must emphasize once again that the legal requirement for the purified exhaust gas with such a system refers only to carbon monoxide and hydrocarbons. There is no requirement for removing nitrogen oxides, yet we have seen that nitrogen dioxide is a dangerous smog constituent and devices that remove only hydrocarbons and carbon monoxide actually might make this aspect of the smog problem catastrophic.

Is it really possible to remove nitrogen oxides as well?

Yes, but not in one stage of treatment. The conditions that are favorable to the conversion of nitrogen oxides to harmless gas are not the same ones that are needed to convert hydrocarbon fuel and carbon monoxide. In fact, one needs almost diametrically opposite conditions: an excess of hydrogen in one case and an excess of oxygen in the other. This is not impossible but it is elaborate and costly. It also multiplies the catalyst poisoning, endurance, and maintenance problems. I firmly believe that it is impractical.

In fact, I am sure that a good many of the most sophisticated smogsters believe that the anti-smog muffler and the Detroit fixes as well represent in the long run completely impractical concepts. The air pollution wheels have been set spinning so fast along this track, however, that they are going to grind to a halt only when public scandal or belligerent public opinion makes it too politically dangerous for the state governments to continue along the same stubborn line. I predict that before 1970 there will be a bursting of the bubble and the people will really get mad. I believe this anger will be directed where it should be—at the car manufacturers.

In the face of a problem that is so vast and widespread and complex and so costly, where have they been? Chrysler has its Clean Air Kit, Ford has supported somewhat half-heartedly some catalyst and exhaust manifold oxidation work, and, aside from the highly questionable "ManAirOx," General Motors has done little more than continue to make money—the most money, incidentally, ever made by a private corporation in the history of the world.

With the single exception of Ethyl Corporation, the list of experimental muffler manufacturers, usually backed as noted by a Big Brother in the form of a catalyst manufacturer or a chemical company, is rather pathetic.

Assuming that now this market will be confined to second-hand cars or trucks (still a whopping consumership), how can such teams, sanguine as they may be, really cope with the essential guts of a technology that is unable to elucidate to everybody's satisfaction exactly how such a simple molecule as hydrogen burns? Let us take a look at just a single aspect of the subtle mess into which these pilgrims have ventured.

Undoubtedly the most serious immediate problem is the poisoning of an anti-smog catalyst. Even an amateur can pick a catalyst that will work—for a while. The poisons may be lead compounds or they may be other materials, but whatever their chemical nature they are poisonous when they are gases rather than solids. If they were solids, they would affect the catalyst very little. After these catalyst poisons come out of the exhaust valves they *want* to be solids, but a strange and fundamental dilemma of nature confronts them. It is the same dilemma that confronts water vapor in the air, when it wants to become rain (and everybody is praying in Dallas, Texas, for it to become rain) but it can't make it. The dilemma is called *nucleation*.

Nucleation is how gases become liquids or solids. Even though the surrounding temperature is well below the boiling or freezing point, gas molecules have to go through a complicated ritual to be able to condense. Great scientists have tried to explain this ritual. Usually nucleation involves the help of other solid particles already present. Molecules find it easier to go through this ritual at the surface of solid particles, if the particles are of the right structure. This is the basis of seeding clouds with silver iodide for making rain and is even the basis of a remarkable new theory of normal rain cycles connected with nucleation provided by the dust of meteors. It is the basis for a classified method for extinguishing the condensation trails of high-flying military airplanes. Yet in all the literature of smog prevention, there is no single reference to how nucleation occurs or how it may be made to occur in exhaust streams fresh from the valves on their way to a vulnerable bed of catalyst.

[135]

This is a brilliantly difficult subject. With all due respect, can we expect the MacAlester Aircraft Company of Oklahoma to have the guns to deal with it? Detroit has the guns all right, but its preoccupation is with "other things." In the face of a world-wide crisis of air pollution caused increasingly by automobile engines, Detroit has seemingly adopted the late twentieth-century version of Vanderbilt's immortal phrase "The public be damned."

The catalytic muffler approach may some day be a reasonable fix, technically and economically, but before that day I believe the automotive scene will have changed in such a radical way that we will no longer need such a fix. Gifted scientists who are deep in smog research, when one catches them in moments of *gemütlichkeit,* ask wistfully about the status of fuel-cell research. They see no future in the Great Leap. Perhaps the most eminent of industrial catalyst experts, Dr. Oblad, vice president of M. W. Kellogg Co., thinks the answer is to go to diesel-engine cars and forget about the catalysts.

With all due respect to Oblad's realism about catalysts, the diesel engine would not be the answer. It is true that in good shape it produces much less hydrocarbons and carbon monoxide in the exhaust. It would be difficult for a European husband to kill his wife by getting her drunk and locking her in the garage with the engine going on a dieselized Mercedes-Benz car. The trouble is that the diesel engine, because of its very high compression, produces a large amount of nitrogen oxides —so much, indeed, that the nitrogen oxides react with the lubricating oil and often cause trouble in the crankcase.

One massive factor lately has been added to the scene, and perhaps the result will be simply to make the confusion complete. This is the passage of Public Law 88-206, the Clean Air Act of 1963. Most importantly this stipulates grants of possible Federal funds for further research.

It is true that the Secretary of Health, Education, and Welfare, to whom the law delegates what modest authority is acquired, may find it just as impossible to do anything really helpful about air pollution as to abolish sin. Nevertheless, the passage of the law makes a thorough airing of the whole matter not only inevitable but possibly endless. It should have the effect of stimulating the manufacturers to spend more of their own money on finding out how fuels burn, rather than facing the risk that Washington, by sheer money, may subsidize enough research to find an answer that would be unpalatable to Detroit.

So far it is the chemical industry, through the Manufacturing Chemists Association, that has done most of the complaining about the bill, although there are bound to be much more serious confrontations; for example, with the industrial fuel people on the issue of sulfurous smog in the large east-coast cities and with the auto industry on exhaust emissions.

The chemists' group would be well advised to keep silence, since it has come out of the insecticide scandals with a public image of intemperate and red-faced opposition to fact.

The steps leading up to a real fight are almost unobtrusively taking place in the hearings, not before any administrative body, but before the Congressional committee of Senator Muskie, the Maine Democrat, who has taken up the baton passed on to him by Senator Ribicoff.

chapter 11

WHAT COULD BE DONE

. . . powers that will work for thee; air, earth, and
skies . . .

WORDSWORTH, *On the Extinction
of the Venetian Republic*

In the face of an almost unanimous expert opinion, although a
publicly unvoiced one, that the afterburners or catalytic mufflers will not work, either technically or economically on
present automobiles, there persists a baseless optimism among
public relations people and politicians associated with the smog
problem. "I feel sure," one of them is quoted, "that we won't
even need the exhaust-treating devices. I have great faith in the
automobile industry. They will be able to fix up their motors so
they won't cause smog."

It is worth repeating that this almost canine trust in Detroit,
if it is based on anything at all, may have been inspired by the
activities of the Chrysler Corporation which has begun providing
quick-fixes for carburetors. The objective is to make them less
sloppy in apportioning fuel to the engine, so that under many
conditions the engine runs on "lean mixtures" (low amount of
fuel) rather than "rich mixtures," which generally provide a
more luxurious increment of power and the kind of performance
the American driving public is accustomed to.

Essentially the Chrysler fix is an extension of an approach to
engine modification tried out early in the melancholy history of
smog since World War II. Because it was found that the highest

percentage of unburned fuel is always produced in the exhaust when the automobile is being *decelerated* (that is with the foot off the accelerator), it first was proposed that the carburetor be modified to allow no fuel to get into the engine under these conditions. The fact that this did not work at all is an example of how little automotive people knew about the physics and chemistry of their equipment. What happens is that, if deceleration occurs after a period of driving under other conditions, the fuel plumbing system between the carburetor and the intake valves has become wet with a film of fuel, and the high vacuum in the cylinders during which no burning is occurring under deceleration sucks this film of fuel into the combustion chambers and pushes it out the exhaust. Thus nearly as much fuel is wasted, whether the carburetor is providing fuel or not. Furthermore, in a careful study of the over-all quantities of fuel exhausted by automobiles in typical city driving, the absolute amounts of fuel emitted during deceleration have been shown not to be the imposing fraction of the total that they were originally considered to be.

The future of solving the automotive smog problem by carburetor modification thus seems to be a pusillanimous one. In any case such fixes would have no effect on the emission of nitrogen oxides and, as we have seen, this would be true if diesel engines were substituted for spark-ignition engines.

However, we must take a very serious look at the diesel engine, for this reason: Since the diesel engine, because of its habitual operation under lean conditions, does not allow very much unburned fuel or carbon monoxide, it is possible to concentrate solely on the removal from the exhaust of nitrogen oxides, which it produces in lamentably high concentrations. Thus we can avoid the impossibly complicated arrangements necessary to take out both hydrocarbons and carbon monoxide (which require an oxidizing environment) and nitrogen oxides (which require a reducing environment).

The diesel engine is very old in concept and, as we saw in Chapter 2, could in a way be said to have been invented by a prehistoric Malaysian interested only in lighting a fire to cook fish. There is no spark ignition in a diesel engine, since the pressures in the cylinders are high enough to make the fuel-air mixtures spontaneously ignite, because as the ancient Malaysian genius found, high air pressures in confined space are associated with high air temperatures. Because of the high pressures, the use of the diesel principle for a long time was confined to massive engines with thick walls and applied to large marine, stationary and railroad installations and to very big trucks and buses. The Caterpillar tractor line, one of the most sucessful of American developments of world-wide acceptance (and which competes as a national achievement, recognized in all lands, with the Gillette razor blade, jazz music, chewing gum, butch hair-cuts, Coco-Cola, and the Jeep) is based on a highly efficient diesel motor.

Recently, in Europe, Russia, and Japan, the diesel engine for automobiles, not only for taxis and small trucks but passenger cars, has begun to gnaw at the pedestal of the spark ignition ("Otto cycle") engine. There is good reason for this. The diesel gives much greater fuel economy. In the European countries, this is a matter of desperate importance because of the absurdly high motor fuel taxes. Diesel taxi fleets have been operated in New York City, London, San Francisco, and other cities with very nice savings in over-all costs.

However, until quite recently the diesel has been too rough a male contraption for the delicate sensibilities of female drivers and American men whose life seems to revolve about the purchase and pride-of-ownership of complaisantly silent and swiftly responsive automobiles. The diesel makes more noise and its husky motor skeleton vibrates alarmingly under certain conditions, giving any driver with the Cadillac complex or one who has had minimum experience with heavy dirt-moving machinery the fearful feeling that his car is about to explode.

That this situation has changed is due to an invention in combustion techniques in diesel engines made by a German named Meurer. He found that the grunts and bumps of diesel combustion, so frightening to the delicate, could be eliminated by jetting the fuel through the separate head injectors (which all diesels must use) directly in a liquid stream onto a dished part of the piston, so that instead of a fine spray of fuel in the combustion chamber, which has a habit of exploding suddenly, the fuel is smoothly and gradually evaporated to give a gentle burning cycle. The Meurer diesel has been called the *"Whisper Engine."*

Although developments along this line will make the diesel engine acceptable to the noise-conscious, this does not make the diesel immediately a competitor with conventional engines. There is the matter of initial cost. Because of the strong construction necessary to contain the high pressures and the separate injectors for each cylinder, diesel automobiles will probably always cost more than spark ignition engines. For commercial fleets of taxies, buses, etc., this is not too important, since the saving in fuel consumption rather quickly pays off the difference in investment. Also, diesel fuel costs less than gasoline. With passenger car owners, the investment is a thing of considerable moment, in which not only Papa and Mama, but the teenagers, Grandma, and even the pastor, and certainly the bank or General Acceptance, play their roles. The big expense for the American car owner is not the cost of fuel but the cost of paying off the nominal purchase price and the insurance. It has been cal-

culated by the Bureau of Public Roads that the average expense
of running an American car is five cents per mile for deprecia-
tion (financial penalty of the investment) and insurance, and
only one and a half cents for gasoline; the rest of a total of about
ten and a half cents goes for repairs, tires, parking, gasoline tax,
and registration fees.

What this boils down to is the fact that the automobile owner
is charged so much for borrowing the money to pay for the car
and for adequate insurance that, even if the fuel cost were cut
in half, he would hardly see any difference in out-of-pocket
expense.

We cannot overlook the diesel engine as at least a partial
solution of smog in large cities crowded with automotive vehicles. But this would require an ambitious program, which has not
even been considered, on removing nitrogen oxides from the exhaust. That this has *not* been considered is an example of the
thoroughly addled state of mind among the smogsters. They are
to be excused because they are up against the most gigantic,
profitable, and strong-minded industry in history.

There is no reason to expect this corporate giant to want to
persuade the automobile owners to buy diesel-powered units.
Why in the world should it? The profits from selling the public
ever-increasing numbers of smog-producers are vast. One should
not overlook the overwhelming *momentum* of this astronomic
profit. When several years of unexampled prosperity are added
end-to-end, the companies not only have more cash-flow than
they know what to do with ($4 billion of accumulated unallo-
cated money that is embarrassing General Motors, for example),
but their glossy executives can think of no better thing to do
than spend more money on making the same delicious merchan-
dise, with changes only in the design of body and accessories.
It is a conservative estimate to say that Detroit spends less by a

factor of about one-to-twenty on combustion research than it does on car body design.

This is not to say that General Motors, Ford and the others are not thoroughly familiar with diesel engines. They make diesel engines, and very good ones, for purposes other than powering passenger cars. It is simply a fact that there is much more money to be made by continuing the line of conventional cars. If the people are crazy, why not take advantage of it? This will continue until a most improbable policeman tells them "You can't put out those things any more. You are endangering the public's health." Who is going to say that to Detroit?

Possibly the worst fallacy of the twentieth century is the assumption that what's good for the automobile industry is good for the nation.

It is remotely possible that as the present fad in cars subsides, and the public returns to sanity in its selection of cars, there also may be a return to an economic consideration of diesel power, and that some American version of the "whisper engine" may arrive on the scene. A large percentage of the cost of producing quantities of diesel engines is almost the same as the personal cost of buying a car—paying off the investment in new tooling equipment. The way of making cars involves vast special industries in dies for casting metals, stamping metals, machining metals, and special hardware production. Changing all this to a better engine, for the sake of public health, is something that automotive executives apparently do not consider.

Here we have perhaps the most serious health problem in history, yet we must rely on the whims, the prejudices and the vested interests of one industry to determine whether we are going to be healthy or not. I believe the desultory attitude of the great automotive manufacturers in regard to smog is a national scandal of major proportion.

There are various alternatives to the present automobile engine, although unfortunately they run counter to the lethal interests of Detroit. First, there is the gas-turbine engine. This has attracted a good deal of publicity, because since the invention of the aviation jet motor, everything connected with this power principle has attracted wide attention. There is an element of glamor associated with the gas-turbine engine derived perhaps partly from its incredible simplicity, but also from the fact that in the air it can give airplane speeds never attainable with piston engines. Everybody can understand a gas-turbine engine.

A gas turbine simply gulps in air, burns fuel with it and expels the hot mixture to drive a turbine. There is no piston motion, with all the complications of injection-timing, spark-plug behavior, and the nuisance of valves. It produces practically no nitrogen oxides, because of low pressure and temperature, and when properly operated, releases very little unburned fuel in the exhaust. In the air the gas turbine is an incomparable eagle. On the ground, there have been troubles, but they have been troubles enormously exaggerated by Detroit.

For example, it is claimed that gas-turbine-powered automobiles have a rather dismal habit of pooping out all the time. Their performance at idling and part throttle has been claimed to be so frighteningly poor that experimental drivers who have driven them have gotten into the habit of suddenly jumping out of the gas-turbine car and running into the nearest drugstore to crouch down waiting for the windows to shatter. The gas turbine car actually is much less dangerous than a Model-T Ford. Its trouble has been that it was mainly designed for steady operation and especially for high-speed operation. Fuel economy was poor except under such conditions.

This is not a law of nature, but a matter of engineering design and economics. By the use of pre-heating of the air through rotary heat-exchangers, the fuel economy can be immensely improved and can approach and even exceed that of piston engines and perhaps even diesel engines. A phenomenal advantage of the gas turbine is that it can burn practically anything. There is no "octane number," as with spark-ignition engines and no "cetane number" as with diesel engines. One must only be able to squeeze or otherwise entice the fuel through some simple nozzles, so it can burn. Probably a sort of indiscriminate kerosene would be adopted, and this would of course revolutionize the motor fuel industry, so thousands of patents and millions of barrels of expensive gasoline-refining capacity would be rendered uesless, but I don't think the petroleum industry would be too much troubled. After all, they are in business to provide fuel, and the simpler the specifications, the better their long-range comfort.

It is of interest to note that Soviet Russia is now apparently engaged in an over-all conversion to gas turbines. I have seen various Russian technical papers devoted to the problem of finding enough fuel for such a program. In Russia this amounts to the question of whether or not the fuel will pour out of a bucket or flow through a pipe during a Russian winter. It seems evident that the Russians, who are as puritanical as and even more stingy than the Scots, are setting up national gas-turbine economy because it is based on cheap fuel.

The gas-turbine car in the United States seems to be mainly a public relations gimmick for Detroit—just to assure the public that "progress" is under serious study. This reminds me of the early days of chemicals in the petroleum industry. In response to stock-holders' questions, even the most arthritic board of directors would report that they had "a man working on petrochemicals," when actually what this man (usually a frail youngster fresh out of Michigan State) was doing was blowing some air through a pot of kerosene and wondering what in the world he had managed to bring forth.

In automotive gas turbines, again Chrysler has been the most frenetic, perhaps because, of the Big Three, it normally makes the least money. The Chrysler gas-turbine automobile is now offered to selected customers free for test purposes. It is a good and promising gas-turbine engine, and Ford and General Motors also have good and promising gas-turbine engines. There seems to be not the slightest possibilty that any of these gas turbines will be seen in numbers on the Los Angeles freeways within the next three decades.

The reason to predict delay is the same one which we have discussed in regard to diesels. There is no doubt that a complete conversion to gas-turbine engines would powerfully reduce the smog problem, world-wide, and that the driving public would accustom itself to such conveyances, but unless such engines take over in a very big way in Europe, Detroit will, in the politician's phrase, have to be carried kicking and screaming into the next decade. What Detroit has encouraged are the following notions:

The gas-turbine car has impossibly poor acceleration performance. If you start up on a green light, you will still be in the middle of the intersection when the red light goes on, and consequently you will be involved in an eight-car collision.

This has been shown to be nonsensical. It is true that the gas turbine car does not accelerate from zero to 100 miles per hour within eight seconds, like a Lotus-Ford, but of what essential importance is that, especially if everybody else is restrained to the same schedule?

The gas-turbine car has such poor fuel economy that everybody will go broke feeding its appetite.

The truth may be the exact converse. With a minute fraction

of the research and development that have gone into automobile body curves, it is probable that, even aside from the essentially lower cost of gas-turbine fuels, the fuel efficiency of gas-turbine power can be made superior to that of spark-ignition engines under all driving conditions. Chrysler's directional turbine nozzle system is an advance in this direction.

The gas-turbine engine costs too much to make. It requires expensive alloys and accessories.

Actually, it has been shown by Chrysler, Rover Co. of England, and others that one doesn't need exotic alloys. The number of parts in a gas-turbine engine is much smaller than in other engines. The simplicity of the design, furthermore, promotes not only cheaper assembly-line practices but easier maintenance and repair.

The grim truth is that Detroit apparently does not *want* to make gas-turbine cars. Their engineers do, but their executives are bound to wring the last frantic dollar out of what has been the greatest bonanza of all economic history—the "typical American car."

There is an even more gracious solution than the diesel or the gas turbine to the automotive air pollution problem—the electric car. So conditioned is the average person to Detroit propaganda that the mention of such a thing brings only chuckling references to Great-Aunt Mabel's 1913 model which she guided with a demure horizontal stick rather than a steering wheel and which could get up to fifteen miles per hour going downhill and which, above all, could not survive more than a twenty-mile trip from a battery station.

On the other hand, some of the smogologists, who know the problems involved in the Big Leap but perhaps have a less clear idea of electrochemistry, think of an electric automobile as one driven by *fuel cells*. Since the fuel-cell concept has been given an enormous amount of uninformed publicity, it may be worth some discussion.

The batteries with which most of us are familiar, including the large ones which start cars and the tiny ones that run flashlights and transistor radios, consume a material supplied in the body of the cell to produce a flow of electricity. In the case of the small dry cells, zinc loses electrons and manganese dioxide gains them, and the flight of the electrons in this process can be made to take a useful course through a conductor in which some effect requiring energy, such as making a tungsten filament glow in a bulb, is accomplished. When all the zinc has lost electrons and has become chemically oxidized in the process, the battery is dead. It goes to the trash pile.

The storage battery has a reprieve, because the reactions involving the exchange of electrons can be to some extent reversed. For example, in the lead-acid storage battery, when it is starting a car, a lead sponge is giving up electrons and dissolving in sulfuric acid, while lead dioxide is gaining electrons to form lead sulfate. The process can be reversed by feeding electricity to the battery, so that lead plates out of solution and the insoluble lead dioxide is precipitated. This is the reason for the term "storage battery"; the device stores electric current that is provided by the generator of the automobile, where direct-current electricity is made by the energy of the car's engine, much as the energy of the water or stream in motion can generate electricity in turbines.

When a storage battery is used only intermittently, as for starting the car, the automatic recharging expedient gives it a long life. However, if electricity is also withdrawn to *drive* the car (as in the electric automobiles), the power drain is so great that the batteries must be frequently taken out and recharged by some standard source of direct current.

The fuel cell is simply a battery which, instead of using up chemical material that is built into it, consumes material that can be added to it and which can be taken along in a tank, such as gasoline, for instance. Such a fuel as gasoline would then play the part of zinc in the dry cell or of lead sponge in the storage battery. A molecule of gasoline would lose a large number of electrons to form carbon dioxide and water, and the oxygen molecules of the air would in turn gain those electrons and become water. As before, the flight of electrons through a circuit of external wire could be used to obtain mechanical power, heat or light.

This idea of the fuel cell is such a gorgeously simple notion that it has haunted electrochemists since rather early in the nineteenth century. It turns out to have more glamor than immediate practicality as a means of producing the power for driving ground vehicles.

The trouble is that only fuels of inconvenient properties, such as hydrogen, and then reacted with pure oxygen rather than air, react fast enough and efficiently enough to give usable power. It took many torturous years to make even hydrogen and oxygen work at high pressures and temperatures in the fuel cell developed by the Englishman, Bacon—a development period embarrassed by not-infrequent explosions of alarming violence, since hydrogen and oxygen want to get together chemically to form water, and this urge to mate is so explosively prurient that they are inclined to skip the elegant and controllable formalities of losing and gaining electrons through a wire.

Ways of controlling this unseemly affinity by operating at low temperatures and pressures with strong catalytic electrodes have been worked out, notably by Union Carbide in this country, which put out a "Hydrox" fuel cell that is being used by the U. S. Signal Corps and others. This involves the logistic penalty of hauling around seperate high-pressure cylinders of hydrogen and oxygen but is better than carrying innumerable battery replacements of the conventional type. The need for a source of silent power in certain military operations precludes electric power generation by the use of internal combustion engines or recharging storage batteries by the same means.

Fuel cells have been developed for use in space and for use in submarines. The hydrogen for submarine fuel cells, now under development, is obtained by decomposing ammonia, which is easier to store than hydrogen. Yet ammonia itself is an excellent fuel for such batteries, as are methyl alcohol, hydrazine, and other water-soluble fuels which make it possible to detour around a lot of complications by feeding the fuel directly to the electrolyte (water solution of acid or caustic in which the electricity-producing reactions take place) rather than through a porous electrode or membrane.

However, all these fuels are enormously more electrically reactive than the hydrocarbons which compose the high-volume fuels of commerce to which we are accustomed, such as gasoline, kerosene, diesel fuel, bunker fuel, natural gas, and coal. Part of the trouble is that the catalysts used in fuel cells are extraordinarily susceptible to small amounts of poisons, usually traces of sulfur compounds, and even hydrogen has to be stringently purified to make it work in a fuel cell at low temperatures. Such poisons are hard to remove from heavier fuels. This is only part of the trouble, since the "saturated" hydrocarbons, no matter how pure, simply don't want to react, and it is probable that even when they do, at high temperatures, it is hydrogen and other fragments resulting from "cracking" or preliminary decomposition that undergo the actual electrochemical conversion rather than the original feed. A few years ago the Allis-Chalmers Company made the front pages by claiming to have run a farm tractor by fuel cells using propane, a constituent of liquefied petroleum gas. The somewhat suspicious circumstances were that hydrogen was mixed with the propane, and alas! it turned out on subsequent analysis that all that happened was that the hydrogen alone had reacted and Allis Chalmers had given birth simply to a diluted hydrogen fuel cell.

Curiously, natural gas which is mainly methane, the simplest of the hydrocarbons, is the most ornery. Most of the research effort to make a fuel cell has been with the more reactive normally gaseous but liquefiable hydrocarbons such as ethane, propane, and butane. Recently a brilliant and massive beach-head has been established by General Electric researchers in this field and the full scientific and technical implications of their discovery are so far-reaching that they have not yet been fully evaluated. Electrochemists and catalyst chemists all over the world are still somewhat flabbergasted by the impact of these experiments, which are characterized by an almost classical simplicity. Without going too much into catalyst chemistry, what the General Electric workers found was that, with an extremely active platinum catalyst, molecules like propane smoothly give off electrons at moderate temperatures and are oxidized to water and carbon dioxide, *provided that a current is being drawn from the cell.*

This finding, which seems obvious to anybody outside the fuel-cell business, must be viewed in the context of the years of fruitless effort with fuels like propane. So complicated did the problem of getting such a molecule to undergo an electrochemical reaction appear, that elaborate detailed sub-projects were set up to investigate each part of the process and this tended to involve almost entirely the study of what are called "half-cell" reactions, in which only the reaction at the fuel electrode was studied, or that at the oxygen electrode, separately, without drawing appreciable current. In very active catalysts a propane molecule was found to sit down and start decomposing into hydrogen and tightly-held carbonaceous fragments that prefer to become a sort of coke rather than give off electrons. The General Electric discovery was simply that the propane was coking because with the half-cell arrangements it was not being *encouraged* to give off electrons, since no current was being drawn. When the exceedingly active platinum catalysts were used in a full operating cell, no coke formed; propane obediently transformed itself to carbon dioxide and water, rapidly and efficiently. (Since this may show the way to run other catalytic transformations of hydrocarbons, many of them bothered by coke-forming side reactions, we may be in for an era of *applying* electricity to many catalytic processes.)

There seems to be no reason why other *pure* hydrocarbons will not do the same thing as propane, hence one phase of the problem of running an engine on a fuel like gasoline seems to be on its way to being solved. It is true that the platinum catalyst is costly and it is easily poisoned by traces of sulfur, and it is also true that the problems of the other side of the battery—substituting ordinary air for oxygen, for instance— have not been satisfactorily resolved, but General Electric has nevertheless given the world-wide fuel-cell effort a tremendous shot in the arm.

It now seems more than a science fictioneer's dream to look forward to a smog-free automotive population based on the fuel cell, and quite likely this could figuratively shift the center of gravity of engine production from Detroit to, say, Schenectady. The chances that this could come along before Los Angeles and its sister cities drown in smog are quite remote.

This remoteness, however, should not be the case with electric automobiles using storage batteries.

There have already been great improvements in Aunt Mabel's silent, slow, sweet-smelling chariot. Storage batteries of greater power-to-weight ratio have been devised; the electric motors to transfer electricity into traction power, which must be attached to each driving wheel, have been vastly improved. In fact, a British firm a few years ago came up with such a spectacular streamlined achievement in electric drive motors that exclusive rights to the patents were bought up by an American automotive company, and the designs were presumably put away in a vault (or perhaps a time-capsule), marked "Not to be opened for 100 years—if ever." At least, nothing further has come of them.

There has been next to nothing done by Detroit with the electric automobile but, realizing that it is the most total and reasonable answer to the city air pollution problem, Detroit has taken every opportunity to make it a permanent object of ridicule. This is not done by anything as elephantine as a press campaign. Detroit has many guns and many whips.

Most of the opinions of young men in the satellite industries which revolve about the gaudy central sun of the automobile (in the gasoline business, for example) are formed in regard to matters like this as the result of contacts with the manufacturers' representatives at the gigantic meetings of the Society of Automotive Engineers, which take place several times a year —two in the early summer and late fall, respectively ("national meetings"), and several lesser affairs, local or devoted to special topics.

Their primary purpose at the meetings of the Society of Automotive Engineers is to find out from the Michigan men what is going on and what is what. The writer can state from experience that the general Detroit line invariably delivered whenever the subject of electric automobiles is broached consisted of derision mixed with errors of fact. It was claimed, for example, that fuel cells were still in the realm of dreams and that even if they weren't, the power they and the motors required to drive an automobile could deliver would be totally inadequate. All this was untrue but invariably delivered with utmost conviction. The resulting impressions become so deep-seated among the delegates that they become part of the American credo, because in their home environs they are regarded as true authorities.

The truth is that with very little development work the electric automobile could be on the road in great numbers within a few years and at a price that even the jalopy owner could afford. It would not be able to go eighty miles per hour, and it would require battery recharging or changing about every one hundred miles.

Essentially the only really revolutionary social adjustment would be the change in the nature of the service station. Instead of driving in to say "fill'er up," you would say "Battery change, please. I'll pick up the recharged ones next Monday." It does not appear that this would be too flabbergasting a transaction to cause anybody to go into a nervous breakdown.

For a while, the cost of driving on electricity would be more than the cost of driving on gasoline, but we have seen that the energy-cost in any case is not a very alarming fraction of the total cost per mile. There would be lowered lubrication costs, probably greatly lowered maintenance costs, lower insurance, and eventually there could even be radically lower *energy* costs, for the following reasons:

The fuel cell in a few years can become a cheaper way to generate direct-current electricity (needed for charging batteries) than is now available. *This* is where the stationary fuel cell could really fit in the picture, until such time as it could be adapted directly to vehicle purposes. The oil companies would provide special fuels for this purpose. Since the operation of a fuel cell does not involve the utilization of heat (as do steam turbine generators), it does not suffer the penalties of what is known as the "Carnot cycle," which limits the efficiency of all heat engines, unless they operate with heat sources of infinitely high temperature or heat sinks at absolute zero. Thus for transforming the *chemical energy* of fuels into electrical energy, and especially direct-current power, the fuel cell is the champion to start with. With the rapid exploitation of such recent advances as General Electric has achieved, one sees the fuel cell coming up fast as an energy converter in central power stations or in widely distributed small stations—perhaps even in the service stations themselves, where they could be put to work recharging batteries for a large population of electric automobiles.

The public would not like being told it has to trade in its Chevrolets and Fords for such cars, but it seems the selling job would not be as hard as one might imagine. It might prove to be surprisingly easy, provided that full advantage were taken of the present car-driving trends in the populations of highly motorized cities. The most evident trend is toward the two-car family. One car is used for weekend trips and the other is for local shopping and errands. This dualism in function has even been recognized in recommended lubrication schedules. The 6000-mile oil drain is practical for a car that is cruising on the highway; it is deadly for the car that makes multiple short trips, and it has been calculated that the over-all average car trip of *all* cars throughout the country is 2.7 miles. Such stop-and-go driving not only requires more frequent oil changes for much of the mileage but the maintenance cost is much higher. (Perhaps the most completely contrary sales pitch ever made was that of the used-car dealer who promised you that "this job was only driven to church and back by a couple of old ladies." *That* is the car to stay away from. It is full of carbon and its insides are corroded away.) Thus, the electric car would be the perfect one for mama and it would be perfect for the car that papa drives to work. It thrives on a driving schedule that is ruinous for the big chariot whose cylinders are aching to get on the open road and blow itself carbon-free.

Would it cause a revolution some fine smoggy day, if the police were instructed to give a ticket to any car but an electric one whose destination was inside the city limits? Even a partial attainment of such an enforcement would solve the smog problem overnight. The reason is that we are dealing with *percentages*. If the mileage of internal-combustion-engine cars could be reduced to that of pre-World War II, for example, in Los Angeles, and kept there, we know Los Angeles would be out of the woods and in the clear, because it *was* in the clear before at the mileage. Since the electric automobile gives out no smog at all, substitution, mile for mile, of electric power for internal combustion power has the stunning advantage of cutting smog out absolutely, in proportion to the number of substitutions. This is not true in the case of substituting diesel power, gas-turbine power, and certainly not in the case of the doomed catalytic muffler or afterburner panacea.

I believe the electric automobile is the most feasible solution of the sick dilemma in which we find ourselves. In the long run it would be much more practical and palatable to the American spirit than the spending of billions of dollars on monorails and other mass transportation systems. Los Angeles had a complete electric mass transportation system once, but nobody wanted to ride on it. It is easier to force people to buy low-power, smogless automobiles (by taxation, for instance) than it is to force them to give up automobiles and pile into monorail carriers, subway trains, or even electric buses.

Professor Fritz Zwicky, whose unusual mind cruises among the stars and the outreaches of what he calls "meta-chemistry," has observed that an unusual number of cars are driven along Los Angeles freeways without passengers other than the drivers. He proposes that such one-man trips be penalized, and that the enormous tolls taken in be donated to scientific bodies for smog and combustion research. He also calls attention to the fact that automobiles not only emit a lot of foul air but they drive through a tremendous volume of foul air. If some absorption device were incorporated into the automobile so that it automatically purifies part of the air that it passes through, he believes we would have less smog. This is an idea not foreign to the one suggested by Justel in the seventeenth century, as mentioned in Chapter 2. It is a good one, and might be worth considering for use on a generation of electrical automobiles. Thus Aunt Mabel's buggy in a sleek new version could help clean up the polluted air even faster than by its simple innocence. It could be an active garbage collector.

Let us close with a resumé, in the way that all respectable chemists conclude a report:

(1) Of all sources of hazardous air pollution, the automobile in urban centers is so overwhelmingly the cause of trouble that one can in non-coal-burning communities regard it essentially as the only source. Pollution from industrial plants operating with unpleasant materials is potentially serious but can be easily policed, and the bugaboo of nuclear contamination, even if it be rightly regarded as a soil effect rather than contamination of the air, is greatly overrated, and is of less hazard than the fact that people pay for too many X-radiographs.

(2) The present approach to solution of the automotive smog problem is doomed to failure for two reasons: (a) it is not based on a sufficiently sophisticated technology, and (b) it is unenforceable.

(3) The sensible and workable solution is a massive substitution in urban centers of the electric automobile powerplant for the internal-combustion engine.

(4) Because of the enormous equities involved in maintaining the present automotive systems, and the fact that these represent the most profitable enterprise in history, the automobile manufacturers will not consider such a change.

(5) The average American has become so much a willing partner in the automotive complex that he may hesitate to accept the analysis of the experts. Will he continue to drive his lethal car, just as he will continue smoking cigarettes?

Bibliography

CHAPTER I *The Nature of Air*

1) *Frontiers of Astronomy,* HOYLE, Harper Brothers, New York, 1955.
2) *Evolution After Darwin:* Vol. I, *The Evolution of Life;* Vol. II, *Evolution of Man;* Vol. III, *Issues in Evolution;* edited by SOL TAX, University of Chicago Press, 1960.
3) *Anthropology Today:* KROEBER *et al.,* University of Chicago Press, 1953.
4) *History of Technology:* Vol. I, *From Early Times to Fall of Ancient Empires;* edited by SINGER *et al.,* Oxford University Press, 1954.
5) "All Oxygen Tests Reveal Toxicity," *Missiles and Rockets,* Aug. 5, 1963; "Eyes Affected by Pure Oxygen," *Missiles and Rockets,* Jan. 14, 1963.
6) "Air"; "Dust"; "Fog"; "Smoke and Smoke Prevention," *Encyclopaedia Britannica,* 1960.
7) "Nuclear Clues to the Early History of the Solar System," FOWLER (California Inst. Technology), *Science 135,* 1037 (1962).
8) "Human Factors in Space Flight," *Astronautics,* Dec., 1961; "Human Tolerance in Space," *Astronautics,* March, 1962.
9) *A History of Chemistry,* Vol. 3, PARTINGTON, St. Martin's Press, 1963.

CHAPTER II *How It All Started*

1) *Man in Structure and Function,* KAHN, Alfred A. Knopf, New York, 1943.
2) *History of Technology:* Vol. II, *The Mediterranean Civilization and the Middle Ages;* Vol. III, *From the Renaissance to the Industrial Revolution;* Vol. IV, *The Industrial Revolution;* edited by SINGER *et al.,* Oxford University Press, 1954.
3) *The Sense of Animals and Men,* MILNE and MILNE, Atheneum, New York, 1962.
4) "Odor and Its Measurement," KAISER (New York University), "Classification of Air Pollution Problems," CHAMBERS (University of Southern California), "Natural Sources of Air Pollution," JACOBSON (Columbia University), "Combustion in Furnaces and Incinerators," ENGDAHL (Battelle Memorial Inst.), *Air Pollution,* edited by STERN, Academic Press, New York, 1962.
5) "Olfactory Receptor Response to the Cockroach Sexual Attractant," JACOBSON *et al.* (U.S. Dept. of Agriculture), *Science 141,* 716, 1963.

CHAPTER III *The Disasters*

1) *Encyclopaedia Britannica* Year Books.
2) *Fog and Atmospheric Pollution in London,* SCOTT (London County Council), *Medical Officer 102,* 191–3 (1959).
3) "Chemistry of Town Air," COMMINS, *Research* (London) *15,* 421–6 (1962).

4) "Effects [of Air Pollution] on Humans," GOLDSMITH (California Dept. Public Health), *Air Pollution;* edited by STERN, Academic Press, New York, 1962.

5) Newspaper and *Time* Magazine accounts (Meuse Valley, Dec. 1–5, 1930; Donora, Oct. 26, 1948; Poza Rica, Nov. 23–24, 1950).

6) "Health Effects from Repeated Exposure to Low Concentrations of Air Pollutants," PRINDLE and LANDAU (U.S. Public Health Service), Public Health Report (U.S.) 77, 901–9 (1962).

7) *Photochemical Reactions of Hydrocarbons with Sulfur Dioxide,* KOPZSYNSKI and ALTSHULER (Robert A. Taft Engineering Center), *Intern. Journal Air and Water Pollution 6,* 133 (1962).

CHAPTER IV *The Red-Faced Stiffs*

1) "Monoxide in Small Doses," *Time,* Jan. 27, 1964.

2) "Carbon Monoxide," PATTY, *Industrial Hygiene and Toxicology;* edited by IRISH and FASSETT, Vol. II. *Toxicology,* Interscience Publishers (Division of John Wiley and Sons), 1963.

3) "Carbon Monoxide No Longer a Problem in Cities," CLAYTON *et al., American Industrial Hygiene Association Journal 21,* 46 (1960); PATTY *et al., ibid., 16,* 255 (1955).

4) "Tolerable Limits of Carbon Monoxide," HENDERSON and HAGGARD, *Noxious Gases,* 2nd ed., Rheinhold, New York, 1943.

5) *Carbon Monoxide Asphyxia,* DRINKER, Oxford University Press, New York, 1938.

6) *Chronic Carbon Monoxide Poisoning,* GRUT, Ejner Munksgard Pub. Co., Copenhagen, 1949; Von Oettingen, U.S. Public Health Bulletin No. 290 (1944).

7) "Holland Tunnel Police Experiments," SIEVERS *et al., Journal American Medical Association 118,* 585 (1942).

8) *Effects of Atmospheric Pollution on Health of Man,* Annotated Bibliography (Kettering Laboratory, University of Cincinnati), 1957.

9) "Carbon Monoxide Tonnage in Los Angeles Air," HITCHCOCK and MARCUS, *Scientific Monthly 81,* 10 (1955).

10) "Danger to Babies," PORTHEINE, *Arch. Gewerbe pathol. Gewerbe hyg. 13,* 253 (1954).

11) "Carbon Monoxide Poisoning in Traffic Police in Leningrad," LYKOVA, *Trudy Leningrad, Sanit. Gizien. Med. Inst. 14,* 89 (1953).

12) "Automobiles Have Not Increased Carbon Monoxide Dangers," PATTY and STEPHENS, *American Industrial Hygiene Association Quarterly 16,* 225 (1955).

13) "Chronic Carbon Monoxide Poisoning in Philadelphia Policemen," WILSON *et al., Journal American Chemical Society 87,* 319 (1926).

14) "Clinical Manifestations of Chronic Monoxide Poisoning," BECK, *Ann. Clinical Medicine 5,* 1088 (1927).

15) "Effects of Combustion Production of Natural Gas Upon Public Health," BECK, *New Orleans Medical and Surgical Journal 94,* 361 (1942).

16) "Chronic Monoxide Poisoning in Finland," NORO, *Nord. Med. 26,* (1945).

17) "Combined Action of Carbon Monoxide and Hydrogen Sulfide," SHTRUM, *Journal Physiology USSR 24,* 624 (1938).

18) *Combined Effect of Carbon Monoxide and Nitrogen Dioxide,* GAISBOEK, *Wien Klin. Wochschrift 44,* 937 (1931).

19) "Invisible Menace in Your Car," DUNLOP, *Today's Health,* Nov., 1961.

20) "Killer on Our Highways," JOHNSON, *Good Housekeeping,* June, 1961.

21) "Gas Chamber on Wheels," *American Hygiene,* March, 1956.

22) "Confusion of Carbon Monoxide with Food Poisoning," *Science News Letter,* July 26, 1952; "Novocaine for Carbon Monoxide Victims," *Science News Letter,* April 15, 1950; "High Pressure Oxygen in Resuscitation of Carbon Monoxide Victims," *Science News Letter,* July 1, 1950; "Body Can Be Taught to Use Carbon Monoxide," *Science News Letter,* Oct. 16, 1948.

23) "Effects of Carbon Monoxide," GOLDSMITH (California State Dept. Public Health), *Air Pollution;* edited by STERN, Academic Press, 1962; TEBBENS (University of California), *ibid;* STOKINGER (Robert A. Taft Sanitary Engineering Center), *ibid;* GOLDSMITH, *Public Health Reports 14,* 6 (1959).

24) "Effects of Carbon Monoxide on Cytochrome C Content of Heart," COSTELLINO (University of Naples), *Folia Med. 38,* 838 (1955).

25) "Combined Effects of Carbon Monoxide and Gasoline," CHERNOV and LIEBERMAN, *Farmakol. i Toksikol. 10,* 22 (1947).

26) "Effect of CO on Korsakov's Syndrome," BILIKIEWICZ, *Polski Tygodnik Lekarski 1,* 1256 (1946).

27) "Effect of High Air Temperature on Toxicity of Carbon Monoxide," KORENEVRKAYA, *Gigiena; Sanit. 1955,* 19.

28) "Carbon Monoxide in Blood After Smoking," CASTELLINO (University of Naples), *Folia Med. 38,* 1014 (1955).

29) "Carbon Monoxide Toxicity in Submarines," ALVIS and TANNER; *Arch. Ind. Hygiene and Occupation Med. 6,* 404 (1952); "Analysis of 105 Cases of Acute CO Poisoning," MEIGH and HUGHES (Yale University), *Arch. Ind. Hygiene and Occupation Med. 6,* 344 (1952).

30) "Carbon Monoxide During Pregnancy," BEAU *et al., Arch. Franc. Pediat.* (Paris) *13,* 130 (1956).

31) "Mechanism of CO Poisoning of the Brain," LEHOCZKY, *Orvosi Hetilap 90,* 325 (1949).

32) "Kidney Damage After CO Intoxication," KOSZEWSKI and KAISER (University of Zurich), *Schweiz. Med. Wochschrift 81,* 1149 (1951).

33) "The Spleen in CO Poisoning," OBERSTEG (University of Basel), *Deut. Zeit. Gerichte Med. 40,* 392 (1951).

34) "Atrophy of Hands in CO Poisoning," ALFORES, *Sewana Med.* (Buenos Aires) *1952,* 729.

35) "Cardiac Stimulation in CO Asphyxia," SCHERMA *et al., Journal Appl. Physiol. 1,* 364 (1949).

36) "Carbon Monoxide Poisoning in Spiders," EPALBAUM (University of Bern), *Arch. Intern. Pharmacodynamie 106,* 275 (1956).

37) "Resuscitation from Juxtalethal Exposure to CO," SCHWERMA *et al., Occupational Medicine 5,* 24 (1948).

38) "Mild CO Poisoning as an Industrial Hazard," MINCHIN, *Coke and Gas 16,* 425 (1954).

39) "Chronic Optic Neuritis Caused by CO," OISHI *et al., Acta Soc. Ophthalmo.* (Japan) *57,* 819 (1953).

40) "Vitamin Metabolism in CO Poisoning," TAKAGI *et al., Journal Scient. Labor.* (Japan) *29,* 647 (1953).

Bibliography

41) "Electrocardiographic Changes During CO Poisoning," GUCHAN (University of Istanbul), *Bull. Fac. Med.* Istanbul *18*, 317 (1955).

42) "Central Nervous System in CO Poisoning," GRAZIANO and GUARINO (University of Naples), *Folia Med. 39,* 457 (1956).

43) "Chronic CO Poisoning Due to Automobiles in Scandinavia during World War II," *Hahnemannian 84,* 174 (1949).

44) "Chronic CO Poisoning of Cooks," URBAULT, *Med. Lavoro 42,* 250 (1951).

45) "Protracted CO Poisoning," BENKEN, *Arbeitsschatz* 1944, III, 49.

46) "Acute and Chronic CO Poisoning," RAYMOND and VALLAUD, *Inst. Natl. Sécurité Monograph,* Paris, 1950.

47) "Concentration of CO in Blood of Smokers and Non-Smokers," VALLIC and DURIC, *Arch. Hig. Rada 5,* 49 (1954).

48) "Cytochrome C in CO Poisoning," MIYATA *et al., Wakayama Igaku 13,* 21 (1961); SPIOCH *et al., Zeit. Vitamin Fermentforsch, 11,* 282 (1961).

49) "Maximum Carbon Monoxide Allowable in USSR," RYAZANOV, *Proc. Intern. Clean Air Conf.,* London, 1959, 175; SHUL'GA, *Gigiena i Sanit. 26,* 3 (1961).

50) "Relation of Street Level CO Concentration to traffic Accidents," CLAYTON *et al., American Industrial Hygiene Association Journal 21,* 46 (1960).

51) "Present State of Knowledge of Chronic CO Poisoning," PETRY, *Arch. Gewerbe path. Gewerbe hyg. 18,* 22 (1960).

52) "Combined Effects of Alcohol and CO," PECORA, *American Industrial Hygiene Association Journal 20,* 235 (1955).

53) "Effects of CO on Visual Thresholds," HALPERIN *et al.* (University of Cambridge), *Journal of Physiology 146*, 583 (1959).

CHAPTER V *The Anatomy of Ruin*

1) "Bureau of Mines Data on Composition of Polluted Air," *Journal Air Pollution Control Assoc. 10*, 367 (1960).

2) "Chemical Reactions in the Lower Atmosphere," LEIGHTON, "Effects of Air Pollution on Visibility," ROBINSON (Stanford Research Inst.), "Photochemical Olefin-Nitrogen Oxides Reaction," STEPHENS (Scott Research Lab., Inc. and Univ. of California, Riverside); *Air Pollution;* edited by A. C. STERN, Academic Press, New York City, 1962.

3) "Bacteria-killing Properties of Smog," ROSE *et al.* (Robert A. Taft Sanitary Engineering Center), *Journal Air Pollution Control 12,* 468 (1962).

4) "Contribution of Engine Exhausts to Japanese Air Pollution," MIURA *et al.* (Inst. of Science, Laboratory, Tokyo), *Rode Kagaku 37*, 577–82 (1961).

5) "Air Pollution in New South Wales and New Zealand," KATZ (Dept. of National Health and Welfare, Ottawa), *Occupational Health Review 14*, 4–8 (1962).

6) "Biologically Affective Components of Polluted Air," ESTES (Baylor Univ.), *Anal. Chem. 34*, 998 (1962).

7) "Mortality and Atmospheric Pollution in Paris," RAYMOND, REV., *Assoc. Prevent. Pollut. Atmospherique, 2,* 381–418 (1960).

8) "Sulfur Dioxide in Tokyo Atmosphere," CHIFER (Tokyo

Metropolitan Govt.) *Koggo Kagaku Zasshi 64*, 1157 (1961).

9) "Application of Gas Chronatography to Atm. Pollution," BELLAR *et al.* (Robert A. Taft Sanitary Eng. Center), *Anal. Chem. 34*, 763 (1962).

10) "Air Pollution from Exhaust Gases in Basel," BAEUMLAR and MUELLER, *Zeitschrift Prävent. Med. 1961*, No. 1, 10–23.

11) Effect of Benzene on Humans, EFENDIEV and AMIROSLANOVA, Tr. Vyezdn. *Sessi Akad. Nauk 1961*, 28–36.

12) "Exhaust Air from Brown-Coal Plants," GRUNEWALD, *Freiberger Forschung. A220*, 157 (1962).

13) "Air Pollution and Daily Mortality," HECHTER and GOLDSMITH (California State Dept. of Public Health), *American Journal of Medical Science 241*, 581 (1961).

14) "Atmospheric Pollution in Paris," BESSON and PELLATIER (Public Health Lab., Paris), *Proc. Intern. Clean Air Conference*, London 1959, p. 122 (Pub. 1960).

15) "Life in Super City," GOTTMAN, *Megapolis*, Twentieth Century Fund, New York, 1961.

16) "Chemical Reactions in the Lower and Upper Atmosphere," *Proceedings of International Symposium*, Stanford Research Institute, Interscience Publishers, a division of John Wiley and Sons, New York, 1961.

17) "Air Pollution," McDERMOTT, *Scientific American*, Oct., 1961.

18) "Sulfate Particulates: Size and Distribution in Pittsburgh Air," CORN and DE MAIO (University of Pittsburgh), *Science 143*, 803 (1964).

19) *Air Pollution and Medical Research*, Sixth Annual Conference (sponsored by California State Department of Public Health, San Francisco, Jan. 28–29, 1963).

20) "Air Pollution and Asthmatic Attacks in the Los Angeles Area," *Public Health Reports 76,* 545 (1961).

21) "Gas-Fired Domestic Incinerators," STIRLING, *Journal of Air Pollution Control Association 11,* 354 (1961).

CHAPTER VI *Tear Gas and Spinach Killers*

1) *Toxicology of the Eye,* MORTON, Chas. H. Thomas, Springfield, Illinois, 1962.

2) "Tabulating the Toxics," SKINNER, *Chemical Engineering 69,* 183 (1962); "Air Pollution Regulations, Their Impact on Engineering Decisions," YOCUM (Arthur D. Little, Inc.) *Chemical Engineering 69,* 103 (1962).

3) "Plant Diseases Connected with Air Pollution," WARREN and DELAVAULT, *Canadian Journal Public Health 52,* 157 (1961).

4) "Effects of Air Pollution on Plants," BRANDT (U. S. Public Health Service), *Air Pollution;* edited by STERN, Academic Press, New York, 1962.

5) "Effect of Air Pollution on Roadside Plants in Denver Area," CANNON and BOWLES (U. S. Geological Survey), *Science 137,* 765 (1962).

6) "Plant Damage by Air in New Jersey," LEONE *et al.* (Rutgers University), *New Jersey Agriculture 44,* 11 (1962).

7) "Eye Irritation in Smog," RENZETTI and BRYAN (Air Pollution Foundation, *Journal of Air Pollution Control Association 11,* 421 (1961); "Non-permanent Nature of Smog-induced Eye Irritation," HINE *et al., Journal of Air Pollution Control Association 10,* 17 (1960).

8) "Vitamin C to Prevent Smog Damage to Plants," FREE-

BAIRN (University of California, Riverside), *Journal of Air Pollution Control Association 10,* 314 (1960).

9) "Atmospheric Aldehydes Related to Petunia Leaf Damage," BRENNAN *et al.* (New Jersey Agricultural Experiment Station), *Science 143,* 820 (1964).

CHAPTER VII *The Villain With the Sharp Knife*

1) "Toxic effects of Low Concentrations of Nitrogen Dioxide, LYKOVA, *Chemical Abstracts 57,* 15454 (1962).

2) "Rubber Cracking Due to Ozone," LLOYD, *Automotive Industries,* Aug. 15, 1962.

3) "Toxicology of Ketene," TREON *et al., Journal of Industrial Hygiene and Toxicology 31,* 209 (1949).

4) "Toxicity of Combined Ozone and Sulfuric Acid," NEVASKAYA, *Prom. Toksikologiya 1960,* 277.

5) "Ozone from Lightning," *Journal Applied Meteorology,* March, 1962.

6) "Ozone and High Pressure Oxygen," GERSCHWAN *et al., Science 119,* 623 (1954).

7) "Ozone Chemistry and Technology," BRINER (University of Geneva), *Advances in Chemistry Series, 21,* 1 (1959).

8) "Reactions in the Atmosphere," HAAGEN-SMIT (California Institute of Technology), *Air Pollution;* edited by STERN, Academic Press, New York, 1962.

9) *Factors Modifying Toxicity of Ozone,* STOKINGER (Public Health Service, Cincinnati), *ibid.*

10) *Ozone in the Los Angeles Atmosphere,* RENZETTI (Air Pollution Foundation, San Marino), *ibid.*

11) "Long Exposure to Ozone at Low Concentrations," STOKINGER, American Medical Association's *Archives*

Industrial Health 16, 524 (1957).

12) "Ozone Toxicity," Stokinger, *Archives Industrial Health 9,* 366 (1954); STOKINGER and SCHEEL, *Archives Environmental Health 4,* 219 (1962).

13) *Photochemistry of Air Pollution,* LEIGHTON (Stanford University), Academic Press, New York, 1961.

14) "Ozone in Cabins of High Altitude Aircraft," JAFFE AND ESTES (Federal Aviation Agency); "Ozone Measurements in Jet Aircraft," BRABETS *et al.* (Armour Research Institute): American Institute of Aeronautics and Astronautics Summer Meeting, Los Angeles, June 16–20, 1963.

CHAPTER VIII *Cancer*

1) "Photoxidation of Aromatic Hydrocarbons," ALTSHULLER *et al., Science 138,* 442 (1942).

2) "Air Ions," STEIGERWALD (California Institute of Technology), *Air Pollution.*

3) "Air Ion Therapy," SILVERMAN and KORNBLUE (University of Pennsylvania), *E E G Clinical Physiology 9,* 180, 1957.

4) "Ions as Tranquilizers," DAVID *et al., Medical Science 3,* 363, 1958.

5) "Neoplastic Growth Caused by Smog Chemicals," KOTIN and THOMAS (University of Southern California), *American Medical Association Archives of Industrial Health 16,* 411, 1957.

6) "Origin of Cancer Cells," WARBURG, *Science 123,* 309, 1956.

7) "Carcinogenic Properties of Exhaust Soot," GURINOV *et al., Gigiena i Sanit. 27,* 19–24 (1962).

8) "Cancer Incidence in Rural and Urban Areas," STOCKS and CAMPBELL, *British Medical Journal 11,* 923 (1953).

9) "Air Pollution Carcinogenesis," WYNDER and HAMMOND (Sloan-Kettering Inst.), *Cancer 15,* 79–92 (1962).

10) "Analysis of Carcinogenic Constituents of Atmosphere," ALTSHULLER and CLEMONS (Robert A. Taft Sanitary Engineering Center), *Anal. Chem. 34,* 466 (1962).

11) "Aerosols and Carcinogenic Substances in Leningrad Atmosphere," VOLKOVA *et al., Chemical Abstracts 57,* 7564 (1962).

12) *Polynuclear Aromatic Hydrocarbon Composition of the Atmosphere in Some Large American Cities,* SAWICKI *et al.* (U. S. Public Health Service), *American Industrial Hygiene Association Journal 23,* 137 (1962).

13) "Tumor Potency of Auto Exhaust Compared to Cigarette Smoke," HOFFMAN and WYNDER (Sloan-Kettering Inst.), *National Cancer Institute Monograph No. 9,* 1962.

14) "Carcinogenicity of Air Pollution in Japan," SAKAGUCHI (Kyushu University), *Egaku Kenkyu 29,* 3777 (1959).

15) "Presence of 3, 4 Benzopyrene in Human Tissues and Urine in Paris," MALLET (Inst. Medical Legislation), *Comptes Rendus 250,* 943 (1960).

16) "Chemical Utilization of Free Radicals," CARR, *Formation and Trapping of Free Radicals* (edited by BASS and BROIDA), Academic Press, New York, 1960.

17) "Soots from Diesel Engines and Chimneys," LYONS and SPENCE (Royal Beatson Memorial Hospital, Glasgow), *British Journal of Cancer 14,* 703 (1960).

CHAPTER X *What Is Being Done*

1) Public Law 88–206, 88th Congress, Dec. 17, 1963 ("Clean Air Act").
2) "New York City Fuel-Oil Controls," *Oil and Gas Journal*, May 25, 1964.
3) "California Approves Auto Exhaust Devices," *Chemical and Engineering News*, June 22, 1964.
4) "Battle's On in Smog Market," *Chemical Week*, June 13, 1964. "Diffusion and Stirring in the Atmosphere," WANTA (Allied Research Associates); "Effects of Air Pollution on Materials," YOCOM (Bay Area Pollution Control District, San Francisco).
5) "Unburned Hydrocarbons Originate in 'Quench Zone,'" DANIEL and WENTWORTH (General Motors Research Laboratories), *Society of Automotive Engineers Paper No. 486 A*, 1962.
6) "Leaner Air-Fuel Ratio, Retarded Spark Reduce Hydrocarbon Emission," JACKSON *et al.* (General Motors Laboratories), *SAE Paper No. 486B*, 1962.
7) "Five Musts for Flame-Type Afterburner," HEINEN (Chrysler Corp.), *SAE Paper No. 486J*, 1962.
8) "Flame-Type Afterburners Not Commercially Practicable," YINGST *et al.* (Thompson Ramo Wooldridge Inc.), *SAE Paper No. 486G*, 1962.
9) "Man-Air-Ox Air Injection System," BROWNSON *et al.* (General Motors), *SAE Paper No. 486N*, 1962.
10) "New Approach to Exhaust Gas Oxidation," CHANDLER *et al.* (Ford Motor Co.), *SAE Paper No. 486M*, 1962.
11) "Experimental Device Reduces Hydrocarbons During

Deceleration," WIESE *et al.* (General Motors), *SAE Paper No. 486H, 1962.*

12) "Engine Kit Controls Auto Exhaust Fumes," FAGLER *et al.* (Chrysler Corp.), *SAE Paper No. 4861, 1962.*

13) "Exhaust Gas Road and Chassis Dynometer Tests Compared," VAN DERVEER and HITTLER (American Motors Corp.), *SAE Paper 486K, 1962.*

14) "Catalytic Converters Must Last 12,000 Miles," DAVIS and ONISHI (Studebaker-Packard Corp.), *SAE Paper No. 486F, 1962.*

15) *The Scientist Looks at Air Conservation,* American Association for Advancement of Science, Cleveland, Dec. 29, 1963.

16) *Alcohol Fuel to Reduce Air Pollution,* LAWRASON (Southwest Research Institute), Society of Automotive Engineers Meeting, Chicago, June, 1964.

17) "Reduction of Carbon Monoxide and Nitric Oxide in Combustion Exhausts," ROTH and DOERR (Franklin Institute), *Industrial and Engineering Chem.,* April, 1961.

18) "California Crankcase Controls for Cars," *Oil and Gas Journal,* Dec. 31, 1962.

19) Rule 62, Los Angeles County (restricting fuel-oil burning).

20) "Catalytic Decomposition of Nitric Oxide," SCHWAB *et al.* (University of Munich), *Zeit. Physik. Chem. B21,* 65 (1933); SAKAIKA *et al.* (California Institute of Technology), *American Institute of Chemical Engineers Journal 7,* 658, 1961.

21) "Nitrogen Oxides in Photochemical Smog Formation," WILSON (University of California, Los Angeles), *Government Contract Report AD 276,* 711, 1962.

22) *Crankcase Control Devices,* Automotive Industries, May

13, 1963.

23) "Automotive Exhaust Emissions," Rose (Robert A. Taft Sanitary Engineering Center), "Air Pollution Control Legislation," Rogers (U.S. Public Health Service), "Air Pollution Control Administration," Schueneman (Robert A. Taft Sanitary Engineering Center), "Air Pollution Standards," Stern (Robert A. Taft Sanitary Engineering Center), *Air Pollution* (1963).

24) "Boxscore on Los Angeles Mufflers," *Chemical Week,* Aug. 24, 1963.

CHAPTER XI   *What Could Be Done*

1) "Use of Liquid Petroleum Gas as Motor Fuel," Swartz *et al.* (University of California, Los Angeles), *Journal Air Pollution Control Association 13,* 154 (1963); Hurn *et al.* (U.S. Bureau of Mines, Bartlesville, Oklahoma, *Proceedings of American Petroleum Institute 38,* 3 (1958).

2) *Photoxidation of Ethylene in the Atmosphere,* Nicksic *et al.* (California Research Corp.), Division of Petroleum Chemistry, American Chemical Society, Los Angeles, March 31–April 5, 1963.

3) "Recirculation of Exhaust to Reduce Nitrogen Oxides," Kopa *et al.* (University of California, Los Angeles), *Society of Automotive Engineers Journal,* May, 1962.

4) "Iodine as Smog Inhibitor," Lockhood (Scott Research Laboratories), *Science 138,* 131 (1962).

5) Diesel engines: the literature is enormous, but I have based most of my remarks on direct experience in petroleum company research laboratories.

6) Gas-Turbine Engines: Here again the technical literature is too vast even to exemplify, but again my statements are for the most part based on direct experience.

7) Fuel Cells: Again the literature is embarrassingly rich, but a good recent coverage is represented by the book, *Fuel Cells* (edited by YOUNG), Reinhold Publishing Corp., New York; and Chapman and Hall, Ltd., London, 1960. One of the key papers involved in the crucial discovery by General Electric which I have emphasized is that of Grubb, *Nature 198,* 883 (1963).

8) *Air Chemistry and Radioactivity,* JUNGE, Academic Press, New York, 1964.